Dear All

Linda Corrigan Baker

KITSAP
PUBLISHING

KITSAP PUBLISHING

Dear All
First edition, published 2016

By Linda Corrigan Baker

Cover and Interior Illustration: Nancy Thouvenell
Interior Book Layout: Rachel Langaker

ISBN-13: 978-1-942661-18-4

Published by Kitsap Publishing
19124 Jensen Way NE
P.O. Box 1269
Poulsbo, WA 98370
www.KitsapPublishing.com

Printed in the United States of America

TD 20160104 200-10 9 8 7 6 5 4 3 2 1

There is no charm equal to tenderness of heart.

— **Jane Austen**

Dedicated to Wilma Jean Corrigan, our mother and friend. Founded on a deep Catholic faith, she loved with a tenderness that taught us how to be good women, faithful wives, devoted mothers, and passionate lovers of life and God. Her example is a legacy which lives on in the hearts of her children and generations beyond. In her obedient, humble heart, she knew that a love story is not real without its sorrows and joys.

— The Dear All Jane Austen Ladies —

Author's Acknowledgements

If you love something, set it free.
If it returns, it was meant to be

—(unknown)

Marie Jeannette Middleton is the epitome of every woman in our large family of creative dreamers and believers who are graced with playfulness, inner strength, unconditional love, and unwavering faith. Like the characters in *Dear All*, we are a family diverse in history and culture, yet one in spirit.

Marie's story was whispered in the hearts of four remarkable sisters long before it sprang to life in text. Following a resting season, fed by faith and prayer, the seeds of this tale sprouted and flourished in God's own time. *Dear All* is based on real family members and experiences, and the memory of our mother's newsy "Dear All" letters which she composed on her world travels.

I offer deepest gratitude to my sisters-in-love, co-collaborators and cheerleaders: Susan Jane Ogilvie, Mary Jean Minjares, and Nancy Ann Thouvenell. Without their vision and inspiration, this love story would not have been told.

Special appreciation goes to:

- Nancy Thouvenell for her inspired cover painting and sketches
- My sister, Barbara Wheeler, for patiently proofreading and editing two versions of the manuscript
- My aunt, Andree Petithuguenin Peterson, and her daughter, Michelle Newell, for the French translation of Marie's love poem
- Mary Minjares and Susan Ogilvie for sharing their insights and close attention to detail
- The staff at Kitsap Publishing
- Bethany Brengan, Editor

Our most precious possessions may not come to us easily, but as Marie can testify, anything is possible if you believe.

Chapter One

Chicago, March, 1924

Marie Middleton couldn't swallow the lump in her throat. The overly-exaggerated waves of her father and brother were in odd contrast to the slow pulsing of the steam engine. "I can't do this!" What had seemed like a great adventure, was now a terrifying reality. Her split-second decision to hightail it back to the station platform was foiled by a stream of last-minute boarders who pushed her deeper into the coach. She honed in on a window seat and placed her valise on the floor in front of it.

Marie hung her head out of the window and scanned the platform in search of another familiar face, but forlorn-looking Pops and Frank, were the sum total of her farewell committee. She was thankful for the private moments she'd spent with her mother before leaving the house. It was better that way, for the heart-wrenching scene of Mama tearfully watching her vanish from sight would be too much to bear. Early this morning, Marie had nearly convinced herself she was all grown up, no longer in need of mothering, but who was she kidding?

A sudden jolt threw her onto the leather seat as the iron horse lurched forward. The increased acceleration rhythmically beat quarter time to her thumping heart and flooded her with emotions akin to her poetic soulmate, Alcott. Words from "My Kingdom" came to mind as her own beloved realm fell farther and farther behind on the Union Station tracks: *help me with the love that casteth out my fear; Teach me to lean on thee, and feel That thou art very near...* Noticeably absent from the send-off was her long-time beau, Bradley Smythe. While not officially engaged, they'd been an item since grade school, and it was assumed by everyone they would one day marry. Brad was wonderful, but he didn't make her tingle like she did when reading a passionate novel; and his kisses didn't make her "toes curl and bells ring" as she'd once read about while snooping through her sister's diary. Even Mama and Pops shared a fleeting glance now and then which nearly made her blush and wonder what exclusive, intimate secret she was missing out on. Although she and Bradley had said good-bye last night at her farewell party, she expected him to be here now. "I'll write to you every week, Baby," he'd promised. He'd also said things like, "How will I live without you?" and "You're the only girl for me!"

Marie's eyes searched the platform with a sense of disappointment, as her view of the station grew smaller and fainter. She wondered what the future held for them. A 2,000 mile separation could place their courtship at risk, yet it was said that absence made the heart grow fonder. Time would tell.

She surveyed her new surroundings before skimming through her well-worn anthology. The familiar words in this book, and those in her private journal, were a lifeline to the only home she'd ever known; the home that was now several miles behind her.

"Miss, ticket please!"

Marie looked up into the stern face of the conductor and smiled. "*Un instant, sil vous plaît!*" She fanned the pages of her book, but to her dismay, the small slip of paper she'd so carefully tucked inside was gone!

"I ain't got all day, Missy. If ya ain't got no ticket, then buy one now or I'll hafta put ya off in Aurora." He frowned, glancing impatiently at his pocket watch.

"It has to be here, somewhere ..." Marie bent over and frantically rummaged through her reticule and valise.

Not Aurora, she thought. *Anywhere but Aurora! I've had enough of Mademoiselle Beaumont and her academy to last a lifetime.*

"Speed it up, Missy. Time's a wastin'" The conductor nearly drove her to distraction as he repeatedly clicked his metallic ticket punch. To her relief, Marie noticed a white triangle sticking out from under her seat—the corner of the illusive passport to L.A.! She snatched it up, returned to an upright position, and blew a stray sandy curl away from her eyes. With a theatrical flourish and a scintillating smile, she presented the ticket to the curmudgeon with a triumphant "*Voila!*"

The surly attendant, not in the least amused, studied her warily as he gruffly grabbed the ticket, snapped his metal punch around it, and poked it under the clip above her seat.

"*Merci beaucoup, Monsieur.* Um ..., I mean, thank you ever so much!"

"Feriners!" he mumbled, shaking his head and moving on to the next passenger.

Marie giggled with delight! If he only knew she was a native Chicagoan who had never set foot outside of the United States! And wouldn't old Beaumont be proud of her least-likely-to-succeed scholar?!

Penny-pinching Pops had reluctantly shelled out a small fortune for her to enroll in The Academy for Young Ladies following high school, where she'd been trained in language, fine arts, and etiquette. You'd think they were paupers, when in fact, Pops was the proprietor of one of the most thriving industries in Chicago, Middleton Clothiers, as well as being financially vested in a few West Coast interests.

Pops didn't mince words over his misgivings.

"Can't make a silk purse from a sow's ear," he commented, partly in jest. Pops had a way of teasing which some people did not comprehend, but it was his way of showing others that he noticed and cared about them. The relentless urging of Anna, his Parisian-born wife, eventually wore him down, and he skeptically agreed to "give it a try and see how it goes." Hugh Middleton sometimes overlooked the fact that his middle daughter thrived on challenges, even if it meant the grueling task of transforming herself from a messy piglet into a graceful, French-speaking swan who dreamed of reducing audiences to tears of rapture with her accomplished violin solos. When Marie graduated mid-term with honors (at the top of her class), Pops gave her a rare hug, as he dabbed a tear from the corner of his eye.

Marie was quite proud of her achievements. While no longer the girl with matted hair and dirty, gnawed fingernails, she was still the same free-spirited, fun-loving Marie on the inside. Not only had she learned to love music, but it had become her passion. It was like cutting off her arm to leave her beautiful Stradivarius behind, but there wasn't room for it in her steamer trunk. She'd send for it soon. Pop's dream of her being a concert violinist had become her own dream—one she'd temporarily sacrificed for the sake of family.

Optimistically facing this new adventure would prove to her skeptical big sister that she was wise and mature enough to be entrusted with Elsie's most precious possessions—her children.

The Chicago skyline flitted by in a blur, reminiscent of her life this past week. Marie's thoughts turned back to what had been a physically and emotionally draining morning.

Marie hummed *California Here I Come*, while mashing down on the uncooperative lid. "Mother?!" Her bedsprings groaned in protest as she flung herself once more across the bulging valise. "Moootheeerrr!!!"

Last to go in was her favorite pair of spectators, of which a lace motif toe stubbornly poked itself through the valise opening, making closure impossible. She shoved the shoe inside the bag, and slid her feet to the floor for better leverage. In the process, she lost her grip on the straps she'd been struggling to buckle. Out sprang the troublesome shoe, and her precious journal. "I give up!" Marie retrieved her notebook and plopped back onto her bed. After carefully refilling her fountain pen, she began writing in her preferred form of self-expression, poetry:

> A lump in my throat
> Tears threaten to fall.
> I pack my valise
> To answer a call.
> What's so familiar
> Will dearly be missed,
> Upon our farewell,
> A hug and a kiss.

The clock's counting down,
A steady tock-tick.
Though still in my room,
Already homesick.

Setting aside her notebook, she lit the candle on her night-stand and knelt in prayer, asking for journey mercies. "In the name of the Father, and the Son, and the Holy Ghost, Amen."

Marie smoothed her long, tousled curls and straightened the jaunty blue polka dot bow on her white middy blouse before float-ing down the stairs in her well-practiced "Gish Glide" ... instinc-tively in search of Mama. At the age of 20, she was hardly in need of a mother, for crying out loud! Yet she felt unsettled, knowing everything was about to change for them.

Anna Middleton, at her easel in the sunroom, was trans-ported to another place and time while painting a French landscape—an art she learned from her Aunt Dedee in Nice many years ago. She discretely draped a white bed sheet over her painting at the sound of footsteps, before turn-ing with a wistful smile and misty eyes toward her daughter. "Are you ready, *Chérie* (Dear)?"

"As ready as I'll ever be, Mama." No longer able to hold back the tears, Marie melted into her mother's outstretched arms. The women clung to each other, struggling against racking sobs.

"This will be our farewell, Marie. I can't bear to watch the train carry you away from me, like when Elsie left with the children. It was *très difficile* (very difficult)."

Marie tried to look on the bright side. "It's not going to be forever, Mama, and I'll make you proud of me."

Anna stroked Marie's tear-stained *beau visage* (beautiful face) and looked deep into her swimming blue eyes, "Ah, Marie Jeannette, don't you know I have *always* been proud of you?"

Marie pulled a monogrammed handkerchief from her reticule and dabbed her nose. "That means a lot. I love you, Mama."

Anna reached into the side pocket of her smock and drew out two shiny coins. "Here, give these to Wilma and Bobby when you get to California, and tell them their *Grand-mère* misses them."

"Mama ... don't hide your paintings. They're so lovely and your gift should be shared outside of these walls. But come to think of it, that's how I feel about my journal, too. I suppose some things are too close to our hearts to be put on display."

Marie's modest mother nodded in agreement. "Who knows, Marie? This one could end up being your wedding gift!"

Marie smiled wistfully. "Sweet thought, Mama, but Bradley may not want to wait for me. By the time I help Elsie raise the children and pursue my music career, I'll be an old maid!"

John McCrae's famous poem had taken on new meaning for the Middleton family after receiving the dreadful news that Jack O'Neill, husband of Elsie, was a presumed casualty of war during a battle at Flanders. *In Flanders fields the poppies blow, between the crosses, row on row ...*

Poor Elsie had struggled to accept the fact that Jack wasn't coming home... ever. She kept speaking of him in the present tense, rather than the past, and continued to check the mail box every day for his letters, which never came. She'd even gone so far as to sail to France in search of him, returning home empty-handed.

Denial eventually faded away, only to be replaced by something worse—depression. The agony of watching her lose all interest in life, often staring into space, was heart wrenching. Pops persuaded her to take on some clerical work at the factory, but she mechanically plodded through the motions, doing what was expected, devoid of joy or hope.

By some miracle, Elsie woke up one morning with a light in her eyes and announced her plan to honor Jack's memory. As much as he adored his little "Woochy," he also longed for a son—something he and Elsie had planned to work on as soon as the war was over. Well, the war *was* over, as of November 11, 1918, and Elsie said it was time to make Jack's dream come true.

She turned to the only logical source, Orphanage of the Holy Infant, where Jack and his sister had been sent following the tragic death of their parents. With the help of the Sisters, along with legal and financial advice from Jack's best friend, less than a year later Elsie became the proud mother of Robert Jack O'Neill III. Baby Bobby was exactly what the Middleton household needed to lift their cloud of gloom. Everyone doted on him, embracing the hope and joy the new life brought with him. His presence sweetened the air, returning the spring to Elsie's step and the roses to her cheeks. For two years the little prince reigned midst love and laughter, until Elsie and her children were wrenched away.

Great Tante Arletta in Santa Monica, having lost her husband of fifty years, sent an imploring letter inviting Elsie and the children to live with her. "I must go to her," Elsie had told them. "I know how it feels to lose a husband. She's all alone and needs us."

That was three long years ago. Bobby was old enough to start school in the fall, and Elsie was ready to support the family through gainful employment. Since Arletta wasn't able to keep up with two rambunctious children on her own, Elsie had written home and asked for Marie's help as nanny for Wilma and Bobby.

It would be a new start—one Marie had not planned—but presented an intriguing challenge she was determined to take on and conquer. She and her sister had a history of head-butting. Being several years apart in age, they had nothing in common ... not until they lost Jack. Grief united their hearts, forming an unspoken truce.

That's what led to Marie's bumpy ride on the rails through one Midwest town after another, enroute to sunny California and the task of caring for her niece and nephew. She'd asked herself a thousand times if she'd made the right decision to postpone her music studies, but there was no turning back. *California, here I come ... ready or not!*

The grinding brakes gradually slowed the train, bringing it at last to a full halt at the Mendota station. Marie checked the schedule, and there was enough time to stretch her legs a bit and make a "nature" stop. The icy March air permeated Marie's lungs as she took deep, cleansing breaths, forming wisps of exhaled vapor. In spite of the cold, she took time to scan her surroundings. A handful of bundled up travelers were moving about the platform—coming, going, or taking a breather like she was. The flat, barren fields beyond the city limits were dotted with crusty patches of snow. Judging by the low, gray clouds, another dusting was on its way. She wrapped her woolen scarf around her throat and shivered. It hardly seemed possible she'd be enjoying much warmer weather in a few days—seventy degrees, according to Elsie's most recent letter!

A woman with a little girl followed Marie back onto the train. She tried not to stare, but noted their "plain" attire. Never before having seen an Amish person, Marie couldn't deny her curiosity. The woman spotted the vacant seats facing Marie's and softly asked, "Are these taken?"

"No, please be seated." Marie smiled at her new companions as they settled in. They seemed rather shy and nervous, no doubt due to the open stares of other passengers. Marie felt ashamed of the gawkers, as well as herself, since she was equally curious.

After settling in, the adorable child swung her legs in time to the singing of a tune, in which Marie identified to be a derivation of German. The mother seemed concerned about the singing and tapped her daughter gently on the knee, as a signal to be quiet and draw as little attention as possible.

Having to sit quietly for so long made the little one antsy, so Marie reached into the paper lunch sack Mama had sent along and pulled out a red and white striped peppermint candy.

"May she have this?" Marie asked the woman, who smiled and nodded her permission. She handed the treat to the rosy-cheeked child. "*Danki* (thank you)," came a sweet reply.

Wondering if the child spoke English, Marie said, "Hello, I'm Marie. What's your name?" The girl seemed confused and looked up at her mother who made the introductions. "I'm Leah Troyer, and this is my *dochder* (daughter), Anna."

"Anna's my mother's name," Marie replied with a catch in her voice.

Little Anna popped the candy into her mouth. At the first burst of its minty sweetness, she expressed her wide-eyed appreciation with an enthusiastic "*Wonderful-gut, jah?*" Hugging a faceless dolly and leaning against her *Mamm's* arm, she sucked on her treat while watching the clouds cast shadows across mile upon mile of flat, dormant fields. Leah pulled hand-stitched quilts from her bag for them to snuggle under before closing their eyes for a nap.

Hours later, the Troyers bid a sad farewell to their new *Englischer* friend at the Kansas City stop, before heading farther north by bus to their home in Jamesport. Marie stuffed a pillow behind her neck and pulled one of Mama's afghans over her shoulders, wondering how she'd be able to sleep in her uncomfortable seat. *If Pops wasn't so thrifty, he might have secured a berth for me, rather than make me spend two long nights in a drafty coach. What I wouldn't give for a nice, hot bubble bath and a good night's rest in a cozy bed.*

"Offer it up!" she could hear Pops say with his crooked, amused smile. In his defense, there was still twelve-year-old Martha at home to be nurtured and educated; but since Marie was not yet in a position to contribute to the family finances, she had no right to complain. Pops was a good, God-fearing man. Though being a firm disciplinarian, he truly loved his family, provided well for them, and made sure they attended Mass on a regular basis. He believed in hard work, honesty and integrity. Handouts were reserved for those legitimately in need. Without these principles, he would not be a successful businessman. *I'm truly blessed, and wouldn't trade my Pops for a million dollars.* During the next two days, the scenery and Marie's seat companions continuously changed. Crossing the California border had been exciting, but watching the parade of one Joshua tree after another soon grew old, making her drowsy. Heavy lids closed, affording sleep and dreams of warm, sunny beaches and swaying palm trees.

"SAN BER-NAR-DI-NO!"

Startled, Marie realized she had dozed off and Los Angeles was not far away. She could hardly wait to see her new home! Elsie's long, descriptive letters of all there was to see and do in Santa Monica had been intriguing, promising Marie she'd fall in love with the place. She felt reenergized and tingled with excitement as she reached for her journal and penned these words:

> Adieu, dear Windy City,
> I'll call you home no more.
> Your crowded streets and soot-filled air,
> Your wintry blasts and shiv'ring poor;
> I leave it far behind me
> For a promised land of gold,
> Where only joy and laughter rain,
> Or so I have been told.
> A gently, swaying rhythm
> Rocks my weary mind to rest,
> Where dreams of sun-drenched days
> Come true, and all are rich and blest.
> A screech, a clang, a cloud of smoke,
> I've reached the western shore.
> With head held high, I smile and cry,
> Bonjour, my new amour!

Chapter Two

Santa Monica, April, 1924

"Auntie Marie, did you have a dolly when you were a little girl?" Seven-year-old Wilma cuddled in Marie's lap while gently cradling her composition doll.

"Yes, I had a baby doll."

"What was her name?"

Marie thought back to the doll she'd received for her fifth birthday—the one with the copper penny hair. "I named her Amy. She had hair like yours, but her eyes were blue like forget-me-nots, and matched her gingham dress." "Oh, she sounds pretty, and I like her name. Did her dress have puffy sleeves? I looove puffy sleeves!" Wilma cooed.

"Oh my yes! She did have puffy sleeves," Marie answered, "and a white pinafore, too!"

Wilma waved her doll in Marie's face. "Do you like my dolly's pink dress? Her name is Susie! We're bestest friends, and we tell each other secrets!"

"I like her dress a lot, and her name, too. It suits her!" Wilma's adoring aunt replied. "Every girl needs a friend to share secrets with; and guess what? My best friend has almost the same name. She's Suzanne, but I call her Suz!"

Wilma's eyes sparkled at the aunt she nearly worshipped. "Do you still have your dolly, Auntie Marie?"

"I'm letting Martha be her new mommy. She loves playing with dolls, and I didn't as much. I preferred to be outdoors when I was growing up."

"Ha! What an understatement!" Elsie, carrying a sack of groceries, appeared in the doorway, looking fatigued. "You, sister dear, were the biggest tomboy, ever!"

Marie cringed, and admitted it was so. "Hopefully, no one would ever know, now."

"Thank God for miracles! You have blossomed into quite the refined young lady." Elsie smiled wearily, setting the heavy grocery sack on the polished hardwood floor.

"Mommy, what's a tomboy?" Puzzled, Wilma looked up at her mother with inquisitive hazel eyes.

"Let's have your Auntie Marie explain it to you. It's a *long* story."

"Now, Auntie, now! Tell me the story!" Wilma begged.

"I think your mother and I have different versions!" Marie laughed. "But in a nutshell, a tomboy is a girl who likes to do boy things more than frilly girl things: like playing stick ball, shooting marbles, seeing how far she can spit, and even climbing in trees!"

While Wilma seemed to mull that over, her brother interrupted the serenity of the moment.

"Chooo, chooo, chooo, clang, clang!" Little Bobby scooted around the parlor floor, rolling his toy locomotive in figure eights, seeming oblivious to the girl talk.

Wilma slid off Marie's lap and planted her feet firmly on the floor. With hands on hips and strawberry pigtails bouncing indignantly, she blurted out, "Bobby O'Neill, you be quiet! Auntie Marie and me are having a *'portant consayshun!*"

Elise's eyes misted over. "That's the Irish in her, Marie. She's her Daddy's girl, through and through."

"Fiddlesticks, Willie!!" Bobby blurted out. "I can never have any fun! Too many ole *girls* 'round here! I want Auntie Marie to tell a *boy* story; a *train* story! Mommy, how comes we don't gots no Daddy, or even no brudder?"

Elsie's eyes clouded, and she whispered to Marie. "I wonder who *he* takes after?" She cleared the lump in her throat. "Children, it's time for your nap. No shenanigans, now. Off you go!"

Wilma obeyed but glanced back at Marie with a "later" expression in her eyes; while pudgy, towheaded, Bobby stomped from the room muttering, "Aw, pooh!"

Once the children were off to dreamland, Elsie put away the groceries while Marie picked up the toys scattered around the parlor. Placing *The Wizard of Oz* back on the bookshelf, Marie thought how glad she was that the kids had taken so well to her, after being apart three long years. She'd been a stranger to them at first, but in no time at all, they were vying for her attention. Santa Monica was beginning to grow on her, and she loved the beautiful scenery and climate; but she'd left a huge piece of her heart in Chicago.

After two full weeks here, Marie still fought bouts of homesickness, missing her family and friends back home. She hoped it would get better in time. Everyone said it would, but Mama's weekly "Dear All" letters filled with the latest news weren't the same as seeing her in person.

"Tea time, Chéries!" Cheery Tante Arletta called to them from the dining room.

The sisters found an appetizing spread of tea, croissants, jam and fresh fruit awaiting them, served on the prized Haviland Limoges dishes. Arletta didn't believe in hiding her best china away in her oak cabinet. Pretty things were meant to be used and enjoyed. Arletta drew the window shades behind her filmy Priscilla curtains to block the bright afternoon sun. "I didn't feel like baking today, so the croissants are store-bought," Arletta apologized. "Bon appétit!"

"They're fine, Auntie, and hit the spot after such a tiring morning." Elsie washed down her first bite of pastry with a sip of refreshing Jardin Bleu.

"Yes," agreed Marie, "they *are* good, but not like yours or Nanette's," (referring to the middle-aged seamstress employed at Pop's clothing store). Nanette had been one of Grand-mère Simone's boarders in Normandy, prior to fleeing to the United States—via Ellis Island—during the war. In addition to her scrumptious, flakey croissants, Nanette had been trained from childhood by France's royal lace makers in the art of Alençon lace ("the Queen of lace and a lace for Queens"). Marie's favorite monogrammed handkerchief was given to her by Nanette on her last birthday.

"So, Chérie," Tante Arletta glanced sideways at Elsie while spreading jam on a golden croissant, "how did it go today? Any job leads, at all?"

Elsie obviously hated to break the bad news, but there was simply nothing in the local area which she qualified for. "Well," she cautiously began after another bracing sip of tea, "I did learn of several job openings, but they're all in the San Diego area. One housekeeping position in particular sounds promising, at the Hotel Del Coronado."

Arletta's cup clattered in the saucer as her trembling hand set it down. "*Oh lá lá* (oh my)! So far away! Over two hours' travel by bus. However would you manage it?"

"It would be impossible to commute, Auntie, so I'd have to move the children and Marie there. You've been so gracious to open your lovely home to us for so long. It's meant the world to me, but it's time to strike out on my own and support my family. Besides, I know there are times when we get underfoot."

"*Non, non!* I've loved every minute of it and don't know what I'll do with myself if you leave. This house will be so quiet and empty."

Arletta stood with a trembling chin and watery eyes as she began clearing the table. She abruptly excused herself and swiftly disappeared into the kitchen, with the door swinging wildly on its hinges behind her.

Left to their own contemplation, the sisters quietly lingered over their last few swallows.

"I so hated to tell her, but I think it's best for all of us; I'm sorry I wasn't able to talk to you first," Elsie explained to Marie.

"I understand. I came here to support you in any way I can, and if it means another move, so be it."

"Bless you, little sister." Elsie smiled affectionately.

"I don't seem to have another choice. Jack's small military death benefit has been delayed pending the clearance of red tape, since his remains weren't recovered. The only trace of him in the plane wreckage was his blood-stained dog tags. It could take up to seven years to make it official, which is coming up, but not soon enough to meet our needs right now.

"It's time for me to stand on my own two feet and take command of our future. The money Father sends every month is a godsend, but I've been depositing a dollar or two whenever I can into Wilma and Bobby's trust fund. I need a job—not only to make ends meet, but to develop some self-respect and become a woman my children can depend on and look up to."

Her sister was surprised. "It's news to me that Pops is helping you, but it's so like him to give to those truly in need. I hate to admit this, but I thought it was pretty cheap of him not to reserve a berth for me on the train. I'm sure he knew I'd survive, and maybe learn a little humility from the experience. I'm still a self-centered brat aren't I?!"

Elsie laughed. "Father really does have our best interests at heart. By the way, Bobby was right about train stories; you haven't said much about your trip. Anything interesting to share?" Marie began with the humorous misplaced ticket incident, described the picturesque scenery, and talked about her favorite travel companions, Leah and Anna Troyer.

Elsie's attention wandered. "I met an Amish girl once," she whispered with a far off look. Within seconds, she brightened and changed the subject. "By the way, Marie. You might want to tone down your tomboy stories for Wilma. She worships you and is so much like you already, it's scary!"

Marie laughed. "I see what you mean! I won't tell her *everything!*"

"I still haven't forgiven you for the Victrola incident." Elsie's face twisted in a wry expression.

"I don't think Cary has, either." Marie chuckled, with color rising in her cheeks.

Elsie studied her for a few seconds, then continued. "I can laugh about it now, but at the time, I was furious!"

"How well I remember ..."

Summer, 1915

Mischievous Marie darted like a jackrabbit across the lawn, dodged the croquet wickets still set from Sunday's game, and couched past the parlor window—grateful for the cover of an Al Jolson tune floating from the Victrola.

"You made me looove you, I didn't think you'd do it, I didn't think you'd do it ..."

Marie stifled a giggle as she reached the oak tree, scaled its trunk, grabbed the same sturdy branch she'd always reached for, and swung her legs over it. *Just in the nick of time,* she congratulated herself. The parlor window flew open to reveal lovely, brunette Elsie Josephine languishing on the sill and warbling, "You made me waaant you, and all the time you knew it, all the time you knew it ..."

Marie scrambled further up the tree. If her old stick-in-the-mud, songbird sister saw her, she'd be called on the carpet by Pops, but his bark was much worse than his bite. Having reached the reliable branch which had provided her the perfect vantage point for so long, she tucked her skirt between her legs and slowly positioned herself until she was hanging by her knees. *Wrong spot!* She couldn't see a thing! Inching along the branch, she made her way there. *Perfect!* She could see ... nothing! Her skirt slipped from its hold and dropped, completely covering her head! *Not now! Just my luck!* Dangling like a bat in a cave and scrambling frantically to pull her skirt away from her face, she attempted to peer through the parlor window. Without warning, her alarmed blue eyes were staring straight into a pair of stunned, coal black ones.

What's he doing here?! Marie struggled madly, attempting to hoist herself back to a sitting position. At the sound of twigs crackling and leaves falling, Charles Hollister, much to everyone's surprise, hastily shoved a startled Elsie aside, and threw his leg over the window sill.

"Hold on, Mimi, I'll save you!"

The situation quickly deteriorated from bad to worse, as Marie heard her father's incredulous voice yelling, "What in the world?!!" Marie grumbled under her breath, "He's supposed to be at work!" Hollister jumped off the window sill, and landed with a painful howl right on top of Mama's prized rose bushes ... shredding his expensive wool tweed pants. Once again, Marie's pleading blue eyes met the furious dark ones belonging to Charles Hollister, or "Cary" (as she'd dubbed him), her father's junior business partner. In the background, Jolson crooned the grand finale, "You *know* you maaade me love yooou!"

Minutes later, Marie found herself doing time in solitary confinement. She glared at her closed bedroom door, nearly boring a hole through it. Of all the dumb luck! Why did eagle-eyed Cary have to show up and spoil her fun? He was like a shadow she couldn't turn loose of. Fuming from the humiliation of being caught with her bloomers on display, Marie had furiously scribbled:

> The blood rushed to my head,
> My skirt was inside out;
> You're a major nuisance,
> I'd rather do without!
> Like a chronic ailment,
> Or being plagued by fleas;
> Your big eyes saw everything,

While hanging by my knees!
What is it about me
That makes you hover so,
And try to be my hero?
I'd really like to know!
Women think you're dreamy,
And call you "the bee's knees."
To me, you're a bad nightmare,
That worsens by degrees!
Weren't we a sad pair,
Looking like foolish clowns—
On the bough and in the thorns—
Our world turned upside down?
You drive me crazy!

Coronado Island, 1924

By mid-April, the sisters and little ones had settled in a cramped, musty room of a boarding house on Coronado Island, until Elsie could save up for more suitable accommodations. It wasn't The Ritz, but they were thankful to have a roof over their heads. Elsie had landed the housekeeping job at the Hotel del Coronado (resort for the rich and famous), as well as an evening waitressing shift at a little diner along The Strand. Before long, Elsie had saved enough to rent a modestly furnished cottage near the beach. Their new home felt like a palace compared to the noise and lack of privacy they'd endured as boarders.

While Elsie worked at The Del, Marie and the children enjoyed warm summer mornings splashing at the edge of the waves and building sand castles. Marie often lounged under the umbrella and wrote in her journal, attempting to keep a watchful eye on her young charges. She'd learned early on when caught off-guard by a powerful, churning breaker, of the difference between the waves of Lake Michigan and the far more powerful waves of the Pacific Ocean. From then on, she had great respect for the ocean, and warned Wilma and Bobby to never set foot in the water without her.

August, 1924

"You'll never guess who I saw today," Elsie announced to her sister between work shifts.

"I won't even venture a guess. Who?"

"Well, I was pushing my cleaning cart around a curve on the third floor, and ... you *won't* believe this ... not in a million years!"

Marie's yawn belied her feigned interest. "The suspense is killing me."

"Well, there I was, making my way down the hallway, when all of a sudden ..."

Marie yawned, again. "Must you drag this out so?"

"There *he* was, and I could *not* believe my eyes!" (She was obviously enjoying herself.)

"Elsieee!"

"Sorry, Marie. I'm still flabbergasted by the whole thing. You simply will *not* believe it, but there he was, as big as life, your old pal, Charles Hollister! He's been here the past eighteen months, establishing west coast business trade for Father."

Suddenly, all signs of boredom vanished. "My *pal*? What would ever make you think he's my *pal*?!"

Elsie tapped her chin, "Well, I've often thought there was *something* between you two. Especially with that cute little *pet* name you gave him!"

"Mr. Hollister is sixteen years older than I am, so you could hardly call us pals, for crying out loud! He was such a wet blanket, hovering around me and showing up at the most inopportune times. He sabotaged some of my best capers and gave me disapproving looks with those big, dark eyes of his. Sometimes I wondered if Pops had actually hired him to be my body guard!

"I called him Cary, because Charles sounds as snooty as he is, and I wanted to take him down a peg or two! It just so happens, Miss Know-It-All, that Cary is a variant of Charles, meaning dark or shadowy, which suits him to a T! I've always thought of him as Austen's arrogant and sullen Mr. Darcy."

"Why should age matter, Marie? Haven't you heard the old saying, "Love conquers all? If you play your cards right, he could be *your* Mr. Darcy!"

"Love? Have you lost our marbles?!" Marie attempted to turn the tables. "Besides, Brad and I have an understanding. We're practically engaged!"

"Marie, sometimes you're too headstrong for your own good. Brad's not here and Charles is. Humor me for once, and you might have fun."

"Fun and Charles Hollister do not belong in the same breath!" Marie countered. "Furthermore, if you're so set on match-making, big sister, how about making a match for yourself? I've seen how Pop's accountant, Stanley, looks at you, but you don't even give him the time of day. Work on your own love life and stay out of mine!"

Without batting an eye, Elsie smirked as she headed toward the powder room to freshen up. "Methinks the lady protests too much! Oh, and by the way, Marie ... I told Charles you're here, and suggested he take you out on the town to see the sights. He'll be calling on you."

In response, Marie angrily tossed a shoe at the closing bathroom door as Elsie taunted, "Temper, temper!"

Charles Hollister had been pleasantly surprised to run into Hugh Middleton's eldest daughter, Elsie O'Neill, also the widow of his good friend, Jack, whom he still mourned. He and Elsie had maintained a close enough relationship that he'd assisted her in solving a personal matter five years earlier.

When Elsie informed him her younger sister was in town, a painfully prickly memory came to mind. After some persuasion on Elsie's part, he'd agreed to show Little Mimi (as he used to call her) the sights of Coronado and the San Diego area. She was a cute kid, although a bit of a tomboy and dare-devil, and had often been a worry to him: setting off firecrackers, performing roof-top balancing acts, dangling from trees ... you name it! He was actually surprised to hear she hadn't broken her foolish neck by now.

"Yeah, I guess it won't hurt me to show the kid around and maybe buy her an ice cream cone or something. I owe it to Hugh."

Why was Elsie so amused? *I sure hope Marie doesn't pull any of her harebrained schemes and make us the laughing-stock of Coronado,* he added inwardly. Hopefully, the finishing school Hugh had sent her to paid off!

Elsie had arranged a late Sunday afternoon rendezvous for Charles and Marie at The Del. Her work shift would be over, and since she and the kids would be at the parish festival, Marie would be free as a bird with no reason to break the appointment with Cary.

Marie made a final check of her appearance in the full-length mirror. Her once unruly curls had been tamed into soft, sun-kissed ringlets deftly styled in a sophisticated upsweep beneath a white satin Edwardian tea (or flapper) hat. Her former boyish frame now rivaled the curvaceous figure of Lillian Gish. A chic white sundress provided a striking contrast against her slender, tanned shoulders and arms. As an afterthought, she pinned a large black satin rose at her waistline. She slid her feet into black and white spectator heels, and hoped she'd pass inspection. Not that it mattered; Cary had always been a tough critic when it came to her. There was no pleasing the man, but for Elsie's sake, she was determined to put her best foot forward.

Elsie entered Marie's bedroom with a burst of laughter.

"What's so funny?" Marie challenged her sister. "I worked like a fiend fixing myself up and don't appreciate being laughed at." Noting her pale cheeks in the mirror, Marie pinched them, bringing a flush of color to the surface. "I'm so nervous, I could puke!"

"*This*, coming from the girl who couldn't care less about Charles Hollister? It looks like you spent all day primping for him. By the way, you're stunning!"

"So why the cackling, Sis?"

"When I suggested to Charles that he meet with you, he said (lowering her voice to mock his manly one), 'Well uh, sure. Guess I can take the *kid* out for an ice cream cone!' Based on all that white, my advice to you, little sister, is don't order chocolate!" Elsie was thrown into a fit of hysterics, laughing at her own joke until she wheezed and tears streamed down her face.

"Very funny! You should be in vaudeville, wisenheimer!"

Charles fidgeted with his straw fedora and picked bits of lint from his white Oxford jacket. He grumbled while glancing at the clock in the main lobby, *Should have known she'd be late.* An hour, two tops, and he'd be free for an evening at the club, hobnobbing with classy debutantes and socialites. Charles had many female acquaintances but rarely took any of them seriously. He wasn't about to get shackled by a ball and chain, no matter how alluring the jailor might be. No siree! He refused to be a prisoner of love. Marriage was not for him; he far preferred playing life's game of Solitaire than run the risk of being dealt a foul hand.

Hearing a rustle above him, Hollister's flabbergasted gaze rested on the most stunning vision of loveliness he'd ever laid eyes upon, poised like a marble statue on the upper landing. He'd make it his business to learn the identity of this ravishing creature!

Marie had arrived a few minutes early to explore her sister's place of employment, but had lost track of time. Watching the well-to-do guests enjoy the luxurious amenities, she gained a deeper appreciation of Elsie's labors (not only to maintain this establishment's pristine image, but to keep a roof over her very own head). She found herself on the second floor overlooking the lobby, and surveyed her surroundings prior to descending the wide staircase. It was, indeed, the most elegant establishment she'd ever visited— rich in history and adornments. She drank in the warm colors of the carpet, the sheen of the gleaming dark wood paneling and banister, illuminated by a large chandelier. Marie fantasized, *I think I'd enjoy being rich!* The Del seemed to wrap its arms around her, welcoming her like a long-lost friend. There was an uncanny sense of belonging, as though this hotel would forever hold a special place in her heart. Taking her first two steps from the upper landing, she looked down and spotted Hollister as he tipped his hat to her with a big Cheshire grin.

What in the world is wrong with him? Is he ossified?! He never smiled at me like that before. In fact, I don't remember him smiling at all! Slowly and deliberately, Marie proceeded down the stairway, heart pounding, with one step at a time. She purposely kept her head lowered to avoid looking into Cary's penetrating eyes. Nothing good ever came of it.

With a flirtatious wink and a bow, Charles made his move. "Good afternoon, Madam! To whom do I have the pleasure of greeting this fine afternoon?"

It suddenly dawned on her that he had no idea who she was. *Well now, this is going to be fun!*

Marie's signature Gish Glide kicked in as she finished her descent; with a haughty lift of her chin, she passed him in cool indifference.

Charles wincing from the blow to his male ego sarcastically uttered, "Enjoy your day, *Madam*."

"And you, as well, *Cary!*"

Chapter Three

Strains of *I'll See You in My Dreams* drifted from Elsie's room while Marie gazed at her moonlit bedroom ceiling, where scenes from the evening replayed in a perpetual loop. The situation she'd allowed Elsie to drag her into, for some cockeyed reason, hadn't turned out at all like she'd envisioned. No, but so much better, quickly turning to her advantage. The lamb led to slaughter, became the victorious slayer!

When she saw the goofy grin plastered all over Mr. Tall Dark and Arrogant's face, her first impulse was to hightail it out of there. But when he asked her name, she knew it was show time! The old, mischievous Marie was back and ready to perform her greatest stunt of all. He was such an easy mark, too, and fell right into her trap. How good it felt to finally have the upper hand with him. *Magnifique!*

However, something in his voice as he choked out "Marieee?" cut like a knife, bursting her smug bubble of vanity. When she turned to face him, eye-to-eye, her defenses began to crumble. In the past, he'd been controlling, sullen, and self-absorbed, but never wounded. He was definitely cut down to size, and she'd felt remorse for being the one to cause such humiliation.

"Yes, Cary. It's me. Surprised?"

"To say the least. I—I don't know *what* to say. I feel like a fool."

"No need, Cary. It was mostly my fault. I was having way too much fun and fully took advantage. You were expecting the old Marie, weren't you? Forgive me?" Hollister had brightened and replied, "On one condition, *Little Mimi*. Have dinner with me this evening! The Crown Room has excellent leg of lamb. You French girls *do* enjoy lamb, don't you?"

She'd coyly tilted her head. "Lamb? I thought you were taking me out for ice cream!" Bingo! She'd lured him in and zinged him again! She'd loved every second of it, so why was her head spinning with such a jumble of emotions? She should be sleeping like a baby. After all, she could easily have refused to go. So could Cary, for that matter, yet out of affection for Elsie, neither of them had rejected her little scheme. Marie finally drifted off to sleep, while visions of Cary danced in her head.

Every muscle literally screamed in protest. It had been a long day, beginning with a backbreaking shift at The Del (stripping beds and scrubbing commodes) followed by hours on her aching feet at Callahan's Diner. Elsie wasn't getting rich, but between the two jobs, she'd been able to keep the roof over her babies' heads and food in their hungry tummies. "Let's take a break, *Amiga*. My *perros* (dogs) are barking and you're about to drop." Her coworker's suggestion was music to Elsie's ears.

"Great idea, Mitzie! I like the way you think. It's been a rough shift. The big dinner rush is over, and Cathleen can handle the stragglers on her own for a few minutes."

Perky and petite Mitzie (Maritza) Moreno, a second-generation Mexican-American, was the best friend Elsie had made since coming to Coronado. Mitzie's warm personality, sense of humor, and slightly muddled vocabulary made the animated señorita endearing and fun to be with. Best of all, she knew the waitressing business inside and out, and was a hard worker who treated customers like family. Elsie would have quit weeks ago without Mitzie's patient training and encouragement.

The women sat behind the counter with their sore feet propped on milk cases while guzzling tall, cold glasses of Paddy's homemade root beer. Mitzie stared at the ice cream freezer and licked her lips. "I sure could go for a strawberry sundae right now!"

"Hot fudge for me," Elsie confessed, "but a minute on the lips, forever on the hips!" They sighed in unison, thinking what a curse it was to be a woman.

"Did the *niños* like our parish festival this weekend?"

"*Si* ... um, yeah, they did! Now you've got *me* doing it!" Elsie giggled. Mitzie had enriched Elsie's life in so many ways, by taking her under wing as a novice waitress and opening her up to a new culture and language. Life in California was worlds apart from what Elsie had known in Chicago. The women first met at Sacred Heart Church, and in spite of Elsie's lack of experience, Callahan had hired her based on Mitzie's glowing character reference. Between the parish members and Elsie's coworkers, an extended family had been formed which the Middleton girls so desperately needed.

Elsie continued, "We had so much fun at the game booths that by the time we got to your tamale stand, all that was left were those nummy churros."

Mitzie was amused by the unfamiliar word "nummy."

"Oh that's just my mother's little word for things that taste really good to her," Marie explained.

"Last year, Mom and *Abuela* (grandmother) spent a few days making their homemade tamales, but they still ran out *pronto* (quickly)!"

Mexican food was as foreign to Elsie as French food was to Mitzie. "I've never eaten a tamale, so I'm curious. They have meat in them, don't they?"

Mitzie listed the varieties on her fingers. "Chicken, pork, carne asada, and sweet. *Delicioso!* It's a long process, but worth the effort."

"I've heard they're pretty hot," Elsie commented.

"They can be, but for the festivals we make them mild, with salsa and chilies on the side for those who like to spice things up. *Muy caliente!*" she explained, fanning her mouth with her fingers.

"If they're that hot, I'd have to pass on the salsa," Elsie laughed and took another gulp of cold root beer; the thought of chilies made her thirsty.

Mitzie teased her, "Why? You have a boyfriend who won't kiss you with chili breath?"

Elsie hesitantly replied with a flicker of guilt in her eyes, "Well, now that you mention it, there *is* someone."

"Do tell! I'm all ears!" Mitzie leaned forward; her big, brown eyes trained expectantly on her friend.

Elsie revealed her secret. "I met him at The Del one afternoon when I was getting off work. He spotted me in the lobby and struck up a conversation. He's a Hollywood agent and said I'm attractive enough for a screen test. Of course, I thought it was a cheap pick-up line at first and brushed him off; but we kept running into each other and I finally agreed to have coffee with him. We've had some nice times together and I think he's interested in me … not in a lewd way or as a means to further his career with my ravishing looks!" Elsie laughed at her own remark.

"You've been holding out on me, *Chica*! Why am I just now hearing this?"

"Well, I wasn't sure it would lead anywhere, but Avery and I see each other at least once a week and are quite compatible. I haven't even told Marie, yet. She's been trying to fix me up with Father's accountant, Stanley Harrison. He's a nice person but not dashing and exciting like Avery."

"Exciting, is he? Does Señor Avery have a last name?"

"Of course, doesn't everyone? It's Weston. Avery Weston! Doesn't it sound delicious and *so* 'Hollywood'?"

Movie stars had never impressed down-to-earth Maritza. She loved Elsie like a sister and gave her a word of caution. "Move slowly, Amiga, and don't rush into anything. I've heard some so-called movie agents operate under an alias and are really *gángteres* on the make for a moll!"

Elsie laughed out loud! "Don't be so dramatic! A gangster? You slay me! No, of course I won't rush into anything. I have my children to consider. And then there's Jack. I know he's not coming home, but my heart still holds on and always will. He was the love of my life."

She paused, fighting to overcome the welling of emotion. "I long for what we had—it was perfect—anticipating each other's every thought and move. I'd consider myself lucky to find something even half as good with another person one day. I have so much love to give and have felt empty and lost for too long—like being sawed in half."

Mitzie snatched a paper napkin from a nearby holder to dry her sympathetic tears.

"*Te amo*."

"Ditto. I love you, too, Mitzie."

The tear-jerking moment was ruined when the fatherly owner of Callahan's Café, Eddie Patrick Callahan—known as "Paddy"—emerged from the kitchen, mopping his damp brow (or was it his eyes?) on the corner of his apron.

"Would ya look at the two o' yas, now? Sittin' there loik the Queen 'herself! Not a care in the world, with me slavin' away workin' me poor ol' fingers to the bone. Heaven knows why I put up wit yas! Shake a leg, lassies!"

Hollister suffered a severe case of mortification, being bested by a female nearly half his age. Why didn't he see that coming? Of *course* she'd no longer be an adolescent, so he should have expected a grown-up version of the plucky kid who used to give him heart attacks and was partly to blame for the gray appearing at his temples of late. The former ragamuffin Marie would have yelled, 'Hey, Cary!! Watch this!!', and hiked up her skirt before sliding down the banister.

Even with fair warning, there would have been no way to prepare himself for the jaw-dropping transformation. Had she not spoken his name—the one she alone called him—he would not have guessed she was Marie. Breathtaking, polished and poised ... and those glad rags! Hugh Middleton definitely got his clam's worth sending her to the fancy-schmancy finishing school. His heart swelled unexpectedly with an overwhelming sense of pride; but remembering the way other men gazed, even leered, at Marie last night, his old watch-dog instincts sprang to life, making his

blood boil. What was he feeling anyway? Protectiveness? Yes. Jealousy?! Horsefeathers!

He'd been pleased when Marie accepted his dinner invitation. The food was superb, as usual, and the atmosphere ... well, the atmosphere was far removed from that of an ice cream parlor! Elsie had been flapping her jaws!

One thing bothered him: why wouldn't Marie look him directly in the eye? It seemed she'd spent half the evening staring at the conspicuous dent in his chin. It made him feel uncomfortable, self-conscious, and vulnerable ... so unlike him to feel this unsettled. Rubbing his jaws, *Hmmm ... maybe I should grow a beard.*

Now that the ice was broken, what should his next move be? Or did there need to *be* a next move? One thing was for sure, Marie Jeannette Middleton had glided back into his life.

Splashes of violet and orange slowly slid beneath the horizon as Old Sol bedded down for the night. Diamond-studded heavens and a refreshing coastal breeze created the perfect evening for porch sitting.

Marie had been tight-lipped about her meeting with Charles, and Elsie was dying to know every detail.

"So how was your big date, Marie? You've been awfully quiet about it."

"It was *not* a date, exactly. Just two old friends reuniting."

"Friends? Are you kidding? You were more like archenemies the way I remember it. No stalling; I need details!"

"Well, if you must know ... oh Elsie! You should have seen his expression! It was priceless!" Marie bubbled with laughter as she shared every detail of her meeting with Cary, sending Elsie into another fit of hysterics!

"Thanks for setting us up, Elsie. I had fun, and found out that Charles Hollister is actually human, after all!

"I would have loved to be a mouse in the corner! You truly are all grown-up, little sister. I never thought I'd see the day! Well done!"

"I do learn from example, you know. Second only to Mama, you were what I wanted to be when I grew up."

Touched by the sentiment, Elsie wondered if it was time to tell her about Avery, and mustered the courage to dive in. "Marie, how would you feel about it if I started dating? Casually, I mean. Nothing serious."

Marie nodded. "I think it would be ducky! Did Stanley finally ask you to go out with him?"

Elsie shook her head, "No. Stanley's just a friend."

"Well, it's time, Elsie. Jack would want you to go on living and find happiness."

Elsie's eyes pooled with moisture. "He would, but the mere thought of even considering someone else makes me feel guilty—like I'm betraying him. I often wonder what Jack would have done, had the tables been turned."

Marie paused before putting in her two cents. "Jack would have been devastated, but would have eventually moved on and looked for someone new to share his life with. It's only natural, and nothing to be ashamed of." She studied her sister who sat silently in a wicker chair.

After a few moments, Elsie made a confession, "You're right. However, I selfishly imagine him tragically pining away for me the rest of his life, remaining true to me in every way, until joining me in Eternity."

Marie offered a non-judgmental response. "I've heard it's possible to be in love with two people at the same time, in situations like yours. Loving someone new doesn't mean you've stopped loving or have betrayed the one you've lost, and I'm certain the new love couldn't possibly be the same as the first. Each person is unique and should be loved for themselves, not as a replacement for someone else. I think Jack would agree."

Elsie kept her head lowered as she listened and struggled to find the right words. Marie broke the silence by stating the obvious. "So, it wasn't only a hypothetical question, was it? You have someone in mind, don't you?"

"Well, yes. But for some reason, I'm not quite ready to tell you about him. Not yet."

Mitzie already knew about Avery, but Mitzie didn't know Jack. Marie *did*, so telling her sister would be harder. Announcing her relationship with Avery would validate its existence and the end of her vow to Jack. Elsie's heart was torn.

Marie took a cleansing breath and bravely paved the way. "Then let's talk about Jack. Did you ever let yourself release him or have you been in denial, holding out, hoping he'd walk through the door at any moment?"

The dam burst, and Elsie wailed and sobbed convulsively. Marie held her close while the deluge of tears did its work. Finally, Elsie was able to speak.

"When the officer appeared at the door, holding out the devastating telegram, I couldn't believe it. Something inside told me Jack was still alive. I'd *know* if he wasn't, I told myself, and wanted to believe that so badly. The rest is history ... how I spent all those weeks with Grand-mère Simone in France, scouring every record, military hospital and asylum, praying I'd find some shred of information to give me hope of him somehow surviving that plane crash. Since his body wasn't identified (many were so horribly disfigured or dismembered, making it impossible) I finally resigned myself to accept he was gone for good.

"I stood where they said he'd fallen, realizing I'd go home without him. There'd be no Jack, no body to bury, no headstone bearing his precious name, and no grave to place flowers on. All I could do was whisper toward Heaven, 'until we meet again.'"

Her voice cracked, but she continued. "I'd wake up each morning, sometimes from a beautiful dream where he was holding me ... so real I could feel his touch and smell his scent ... with the crushing realization he was dead. I'd turn to tell him something, only to find an empty chair. I'd ask myself, 'How will I get through today, let alone the rest of my life, without him?' It seemed humanly impossible and sometimes I wanted to fall asleep and wake up with Jack in Heaven. You see, I really did want to die, but there was Wilma to think of. Eventually, with the love of family and faith in God, I kept moving forward one day at a time, no longer asking how I'd get through each one."

Marie dabbed at her own stream of tears, as Elsie continued. "Sister Faith was a real lifeline for me during my darkest days. Being Jack's only sibling, her grief was as fresh and raw as mine, but she'd patiently listen to me through my looniest moments when I ranted and raved. Sometimes, all we did was cry together. Then she would calmly and wisely offer healing words of strength and encouragement. They were usually the very words I needed at the moment. No matter how many times I showed up at the Holy Infant, Faith made time and room for me, and loved me. She gave me what I needed most: an empathizing heart."

Marie nasally interjected, "I met Sister Faith at your wedding, and instantly sensed her deep devotion to God and family, and her depth of wisdom. I liked her right off the bat."

Elsie nodded and continued. "She's all of that and more to me. Of course I had Wilma to bring me joy. Bobby came later so Jack didn't know about him, but he's as much a part of Jack as Wilma is. Without my children, I shudder to think what might have become of me. They keep him alive. A part of *me* died that day, too ... a part that's buried somewhere in France with Jack. I'll never love anyone the way I love Jack."

"You mean the way you *loved* Jack, right?" Marie asked.

"No, sis. That wasn't a slip of the tongue. I'll never stop loving Jack!"

Tears continued to fall until the two were drained.

"Let's call it a night, Elsie. You need your rest, but thanks for opening your heart to me. We haven't talked like this before. You normally tend to cover what's going on inside with a mask of bravery or by cracking jokes ... bad jokes, too, I might add!"

Elsie brightened and gave Marie a good-night squeeze. "I love you, sweetie, and could not survive without you."

Sleep eluded Marie that night. She tried to write, but there weren't enough adjectives to describe the depth of her sister's pain and loss. Her memory returned to that fateful day.

Chicago, November, 1917

"Please make her stop!" Marie buried her head under a down-filled pillow, knowing her plea would go unheard since she was alone in the attic to which she'd been banished for the past six months. Her own room was now a nursery for her baby niece, Wilma, who was loudly crying for a diaper change and feeding. She loved the child dearly, but her constant demands for attention were too much to bear. Marie felt neglected and cast aside, as though her own needs and plans meant nothing.

America was at war, Marie reminded herself. Elsie's husband was a serviceman in harm's way, far off in France. Sacrificing her own comfort was the least she could do for the war effort. In her heart, she knew that was true, and felt guilty for indulging in self-pity. Flipping onto her back, Marie frowned at the limp curtain ... not a flutter at the tiny window. Maybe this *Yacki Hacki Wicki Wacki Woo* song would coax in a tropical breeze to the stuffy attic, where the heat from the downstairs radiators had risen. Adding to the din was the incessant barking of the family's beloved dog, Isabella.

In rhythm to the blaring music floating up from the parlor Victrola, Marie sashayed toward the window, imagining herself on a beach in Honolulu. Pushing the curtain aside, she watched a bicycle turn the corner at the end of their block. An eerie foreboding gripped her heart as the uniformed rider passed one house, then another, and another. "Don't stop. Please don't stop!"

Marie spun around and bolted for the attic door, flung it open and raced to the stairs. The record ended. Silence. Isabella's mournful howl sent a chill down Marie's spine. She flew down the flight of stairs, praying all would be well by the time she reached the bottom. Then it came. The last sound she wanted to hear vibrated her eardrums ... the doorbell.

Hours later, the Victrola lid was closed, the dog had stopped barking, and baby Wilma was being cuddled by her grand-mère. But there was no comforting Elsie; her woeful sobs were heart-wrenching. Marie was tortured with the memory of her selfish attitude and by knowing there was nothing she could do to make her sister's pain go away. Why couldn't she wail and moan and cry like the others? It might help, but numbing fear paralyzed her. In shame, she retreated to the solace of her attic room, hoping to escape the echoes of grief and to privately mourn in the language she knew best:

> The house is draped in silence,
> The pendulum stands still,
> Muffled footsteps
> Cross the floor,
> Since death knocked
> At our door.
> A gold star ringed with laurel,
> Upon our window pane;
> A morbid wreath,
> Black as war,
> Since death knocked
> At our door.
> Oppressive and unyielding,
> Grief hangs midst stagnant air.
> He won't come home . . .
> Nevermore . . .
> Since death knocked
> At our door.

Though seven years had passed, it seemed like yesterday. At times like tonight, the pain was fresh and raw. Oddly, something deep inside of her understood Elsie's declaration, "I will never love anyone the way I love Jack."

Chapter Four

Coronado, California, Summer 1924

Callahan's was filled to capacity. The rank odor of cabbage boiling in Paddy's huge kettles never seemed to hurt business at The Silver Strand's very popular Irish cafe.

Stanley Harrison, trusted accountant for Hugh Middleton's west coast interests, sipped on a glass of ice water while perusing the latest headlines in the *San Diego Sun*. After glancing across the dining room, covertly observing his favorite waitress finish up with the table ahead of his, he buried his nose back in the paper and pretended to read. Seeing her was the best part of his humdrum day of numbers crunching and gave him something refreshing to look forward to. At last she approached, order pad and pencil at the ready. "Good evening, Stanley! What will it be tonight? The usual?"

Stanley neatly folded his newspaper, removed his round-rimmed spectacles, and smiled.

"Good evening to you, too, Mrs. O'Neill! Yes, I'm quite the creature of habit. The usual, please! Can't seem to live without it." (*Or without you,* he thought.)

"Okey dokey! One order of Irish stew and a slice of apple amber coming right up! And Stanley, we've known each other for years. Please call me Elsie!"

Stanley's light complexion flushed slightly, "If you insist ... Elsie. I hold you in the highest regard and wouldn't intentionally disrespect you in any way, ma'am."

"I know, Stanley, you're one in a million; I trust you like my own brother!"

Elsie turned to place the order, leaving Stanley gazing with a mixture of pain and longing at her graceful frame, and glossy brown hair which she'd neatly twisted into a bun at the nape of her lovely neck.

Mitzie grabbed Elsie's arm in passing and whispered raspily, "I like this one!"

"Why Mitzie! Won't Paulo be insanely jealous if he finds out?!" Elsie jested with mock astonishment.

"You know what I mean, Chica. For you! Not for me!"

Elsie impatiently rolled her eyes, sighing. "Mitz, we've been over this before. You know how attracted I am to Avery. Granted, Stanley Harrison's as nice as they come and will make some girl very happy one day, but I'm not interested in him for myself. He seems rather timid and boring. Avery Weston makes me feel alive and can take me places I never even dreamed of. I thought my life was complete just being a good wife and mother, but Avery has widened my view of the world. There's so much out there to explore, and Avery has offered to lead the way."

"I'm sure you think Señior Weston can make you happy, but from what I've seen, there's only one girl who can make *this* guy happy—you!" Mitzie jerked her head in Stanley's direction. "He's sitting over there looking at you like a love-sick *cachorro* (puppy)."

"End of conversation. I have no time for this!" Elsie pressed her lips firmly together with a "lay off" expression.

Paddy's bellowing voice put an end to the uncomfortable standoff. "Don't be dilly-dallyin' now!"

Nearly tripping over Bobby's toy biplane (a recent birthday gift from his Uncle Frank), Marie raced into the kitchen and grabbed the receiver.

"Hello?!"

"Hey, Marie, that you, Baby?"

Baby? Of all the nerve! The voice sounded vaguely familiar.

"Um ... who *is* this?!"

"Why, it's me! Brad!"

Marie almost asked "Brad Who?" but suddenly the light bulb flashed on. *Bradley Smythe.*

"Brad! How are you?" What on Earth could he want after all this time, and nothing more than a few mundane letters. At least he'd apologized for not showing up at the train departure; his car had broken down on the way to the depot.

"I'm great, but I don't have much time. Catching a train in a few minutes."

"That's nice ... where're you headed?"

"Well, ya see ... that's why I'm calling. Not much time, so I'll make it snappy. I've been doing a lot of thinking lately ... about us ... and it's time we talked in person." (The line crackled.)

"I didn't quite catch all of that, Brad. If you're in a hurry, I guess you'll have to call back at a better time."

Stammering, "Uh, well, no ... ya see, like I said, that's why I'm calling. I'm on my way *there* ... to sunny California!"

Marie was silent.

"You still there, Marie?" (More crackling.)

"Yes, Brad. I'm here, but we seem to have a bad connection. Did you say you're on your way *here*?"

"That's right! I'll be in L.A. Sunday morning and will grab the first bus to your neck of the woods. Figure I'll be there by noon. Where should we meet for lunch?"

Her head was spinning. Granted, he *was* calling long distance on a poor line connection so needed to be brief, but this was all too sudden. She supposed she could fit Brad in after her brunch date with Cary, since Elsie had the entire day off.

"I was thinking about that fancy hotel you've got there, the Del Colorado, or something?"

"It's *Coronado*, but no, that wouldn't work ..." (anywhere but The Del, where Cary was staying). "The Coronado Boathouse across from The Del would be better. You can't miss it. How about meeting me there?"

"Great! I'll see ya at twelve o'clock, sharp!"

"Uh, Brad ... could we make it a little bit later? Around twelve-thirty?"

"Great! Gotta scram, Baby! Bye!"

"Bye, Brad, nice talk . . ."

Click!

What could this mean? Was he actually coming to pop the question after all this time? If so, shouldn't she be ecstatic? Bradley was a solid, steady young man with a good head on his shoulders. He would provide well for his family, and she was sure he'd be a faithful and loving husband. He'd treated her with respect, and she felt comfortable with him. He'd been thinking about her, but Marie had to admit it had been awhile since Brad had crossed her mind in a romantic way. To her surprise, a vision of Cary popped into her head, making her tingle all over. Brad had never made her feel that way. *But tingly doesn't last forever, and dependability does*, she reasoned. She had a lot of soul-searching to do during the next few days.

Bobby O'Neill squirmed in the chair as the frustrated barber tried to clip his overgrown hair. Elsie had put the trim off as long as possible, dreading the battle which was sure to ensue.

"Pooh! I don't wanna get my hair cut! I *hate* haircuts!"

In desperation, Elsie did what any mother at her wits end would do—resorted to bribery! "If you sit still like a good boy, we'll have a picnic later at the dock and watch the boats."

It worked! "Awright, Mommy. I *like* boats!" The little scamp sat still as a possum, ready to endure the "ear lowering" procedure.

"And don't say *pooh*, Bobby O'Neill! That's a bad word!" Wilma scolded her little brother while glancing at their mother for affirmation.

Snipping away with skilled precision, the seasoned barber squinted at Bobby's reflection in the mirror and over at Wilma, who kept coughing from the cloying mingled scents of sandalwood, bay rum and Barbicide which hung heavily in the close quarters of the tonsorial establishment.

"You'd never know they was brother and sister. Don't look nuthin' alike. And the boy don't favor you a'tall, neither, ma'am."

Instantly, Elsie's hackles were raised, and she spit out in a defensive tone, "They most certainly *are* brother and sister; and I can assure you, sir, both of them, including 'the boy,' are mine!" Elsie wished others would keep their comments to themselves, especially in front of the children. *We won't be coming here again!*

Breathing in the salty air was a soothing balm for Elsie's inflamed nerves. *I shouldn't let ignorant people push my buttons,* she chided herself. She made it a priority to spend her days off with the children and give Marie some well-deserved time to herself. A stroll along the pier with her little ones was good medicine any day of the week. The muffled thump-thump of hulls bouncing against the dock, calls of hungry seagulls, the stinky odor of kelp, and the clanging of a distant buoy bell created a tranquil environment for the weary, single mother.

"Look, Mommy! I've seen that man over there before. You have a picture of him with Daddy, don't you?" Wilma pointed toward a Skerry Cruiser which had pulled into its berth a moment before—where sure enough, Charles Hollister, dressed to the nines in yachting apparel, was tying up.

Bobby jumped up and down on restless, chubby legs. "Let's go over dere! I wanna see da boat! I wanna ride in it!"

"I get to go, too, Bobby!" Wilma had no intention of being left behind.

Bobby puffed out his chest with an air of manly authority and stretched himself to his full three-foot, four-inch height. "Naw, Willie, boats are for *boys!*"

Elsie began leading her squabbling children in Hollister's direction, but came to an abrupt halt. A stylish woman gingerly emerged from the wobbly vessel. Hollister attentively assisted her, then protectively slipped her hand through his arm and led her to the boardwalk.

Elsie squinted against the bright sun and muttered, "Who is *she*?!"

It was Hollister's turn to freeze in place. With a slightly sheepish attempt at a smile, he looked for all the world as if he'd been caught with his hand in the cookie jar.

"Can I see your boat, Mister? Can I?" bouncy Bobby begged.

Hollister patted the tyke on top of his platinum blond head. "I'm sorry, son. Not today, but we'll do it another time, soon." Then making a motion on his chest with his right hand, "Cross my heart."

"An' hope ta die?"

"An' hope ta die!"

"Deal!" Bobby stuck out his tongue at Wilma, and she kicked him in the shins. They began pummeling each other, while the strange woman looked down on them in astonishment.

"Children! Stop it this instant!" their chagrined mother demanded. Elsie placed a firm hand on each child's shoulder, prying them apart to prevent the scuffle from further escalation.

Elsie had never known Charles Hollister to appear vulnerable, yet he looked like a fish out of water. It certainly did not become his signature debonair image. Noticeably flustered, Hollister yanked the handkerchief from his breast pocket and swiped at a red blotch on the corner of his mouth.

After an awkward pause, he found his voice, "May I introduce you two ladies?" The woman at his side was Jayne Blackwell, a business acquaintance.

Upon learning that Elsie was Hugh's eldest daughter, Miss Blackwell spoke with a pretentious air, "So, you're a Middleton, then, are you? I do recall hearing a little something about the family. I believe you have a little sister who is a bit of a tomboy, don't you?" A trickle of smoke from the woman's Lucky Strike cigarette trickled through her slightly-smudged scarlet lips.

Elsie sized up the socialite and self-consciously compared her own frumpy gingham morning dress to Miss Blackwell's in-vogue nautical costume, before curtly replying, "I *do* have two younger sisters, but neither is a tomboy. The oldest of the two, Marie, lives with us and is my children's nanny," glancing at Charles with questioning eyes.

Hollister seemed reluctant to look Elsie directly in the eye and flushed at the mention of Marie's name.

Miss Blackwell's forced smile faded. "Hadn't we best be going, Darling? My chauffeur is waiting."

"Um, yes. I suppose so."

Then Charles addressed Elsie with an apologetic air, "Nice running into you, Elsie; I *will* make a boating date with the kiddies soon. Enjoy the rest of your afternoon."

"You, as well, Charles." Elsie's eyes followed the pair as they continued arm-in-arm along the boardwalk, wishing she hadn't meddled in her sister's love life.

To Elsie's dismay, Bobby blabbed his boat story to Marie as soon as he walked in the door. Thankfully, he'd left out the part about Jayne Blackwell.

Smiling brightly at her sister, "You saw Cary today?" Marie asked.

Elsie gulped, not able to return the smile. "Yes, at the dock after Bobby's haircut. I took the kids down there for a little picnic, and Charles pulled into port as we were admiring the boats."

"And he had a really beauuu-tee-ful lady with him!" chimed in Wilma.

Elsie and Marie simultaneously turned pale. Giving her sister a sympathetic pat on the shoulder, Elsie said, "We'll talk later, Sis."

Before retiring, Marie wondered if Cary planned to keep their Sunday brunch date, and asked herself the burning question:

> Who says I have to fall in love?
> It seems the thing to do;
> Choose a sweetheart—a matching glove,
> Then cuddle and bill and coo.
> Who says there's someone made for me,
> When I'm just fine on my own?
> Maybe that's how it's meant to be—
> A peaceful life, all alone.
> Who says I have to be like them:
> The ones with joy and laughter,
> And love so real it never ends . . .
> Happily ever after?
> Who says I need to find the one
> Who'll make all my dreams come true?
> Who says I have to fall in love?
> Maybe—just maybe—*I* do.

Chapter Five

Hotel del Coronado, late August, 1924

"Cary, who is that woman on the veranda?" lightly inquired Marie while looking toward the high waterfront windows of the seaside lounge.

This was Hollister's first engagement with Marie since the ice cream cone incident. Although Charles still cringed with embarrassment over his blunder, they had formed a friendly truce and were becoming better acquainted. Earlier, Miss Blackwell had invited him to her table and was openly disappointed upon learning of his brunch date with "the little tomboy."

Now following Marie's gaze, he locked eyes with Jayne. Her raven hair and peaches and cream skin reminded him of the attraction he first felt when they met in Boston two years earlier. That attraction had not diminished. Her beauty coupled with brains was a combination lacking in the other women he associated with. However, the lovely, savvy young lady seated across with him was definitely growing on him.

"Did you hear me, Cary?" Marie interrupted Hollister's preoccupation with Jayne.

He returned his attention to Marie with a provoking grin, "Are you referring to the dark-haired woman over there with the alluring brown eyes who's staring us down? She's Jayne Blackwell of the Boston Blackwells."

Detecting Marie's uneasiness, he inwardly congratulated himself for regaining the upper hand. Much to his satisfaction and restored male ego, the two women had obviously noticed each other, and neither seemed pleased. Charles leaned toward Marie, his voice a raspy whisper, "She asked the same of you earlier this morning, Mimi!"

Marie tried to make light of Charles's comment, as he observed her with amusement dancing in his ebony eyes. "Not that it's of any consequence to me, whatsoever, but I was wondering ... since she keeps watching you ... if she's one of your business associates."

Hollister inwardly chuckled as Marie appeared to be holding her breath, waiting for his answer. "Well, yes ... and no." He glanced from Marie's tense expression back to Jayne, who was now engaged in close conversation with her own brunch companion.

"Miss Blackwell's father, Milton, does business with our firm, and we first met in Boston to close a deal. I was invited to a dinner gathering at his club where he introduced me to his daughter. She and I quickly discovered common ground and compared stories of our travels and alma maters: she graduated from William and Mary the same year that I graduated from the University of Chicago. Jayne gave me some good leads for my buying trips, since she's an art historian with exquisite taste in fashion." He studied Marie with smug satisfaction. His words had definitely made an impact.

"So what did you say about me when she asked, if she *did* ask?" Marie looked jittery, as though fighting to keep a steady hand while sipping her iced tea.

"Well, she wondered if you were my kid sister. I told her it was worse than that, and gave her a detailed explanation of how I found you one day hanging upside down in a tree, felt sorry for you, and took you under my wing for etiquette and deportment lessons," teased Hollister.

"You did *not!*" Marie narrowed her eyes into a squinty anger which didn't quite match the slight smirk at the corner of her mouth. Charles threw his head back and laughed, amused that he'd gotten under her sensitive skin.

Charles watched his fetching date cut her fruit into dainty, bite-sized pieces, while he absentmindedly stirred his Virgin Bloody Mary with a celery stick. Mimi had grown up, but was still as vulnerable as a little girl ... and spunky, too. He liked that! He couldn't help comparing her to Miss Blackwell. Jayne was far more confident, poised, articulate, and well-educated. He found her fascinating, yet was keeping all females at arm's length. Since that business trip to Boston, he and Jayne had gone their separate ways until she'd registered at The Del last week. A warm greeting of surprise and pleasantries had led to a tentative dinner engagement.

"Don't look now, but she's on her way over here!" whispered Marie, ending his preoccupation. When the woman was within feet of their table, Marie nonchalantly fidgeted with her long strand of beads.

Hollister stood with a slight bow as Miss Blackwell reached their table and gaily offered her hand to his. "Jayne Blackwell, I'd like to introduce you to Miss Marie Middleton of Chicago."

Jayne forced a red-tinted smile that did not quite reach her eyes. "We meet, at last, Miss Middleton. I've heard so *much* about you! Are you enjoying the California sunshine and culture?"

Marie flashed a phony-looking smile in return, "I am, indeed, Miss Blackwell. How long are you planning to be in town?"

"Through autumn, at the very least, should I be persuaded to stay." Jayne turned her smoky eyes toward Hollister. "Perhaps through winter, since the frigid Boston weather drives me to warmer climes during the season. Can you imagine my delight at finding my dear friend, Charles, here for the season, as well?!"

Marie's smile faded when Cary beamed at Miss Blackwell and nodded in agreement.

With a condescending smile, Jayne asked, "How about you, Miss Middleton? Are you passing through on your way back to school, dear?"

Marie straightened her spine, sat slightly taller in her oversized chair, and replied with an icy edge to her voice, "I am *not* a school girl, Miss Blackwell, and will be living in Coronado *indefinitely*. I was also surprised," she curtly added, "to see *my* dear, old friend, Charles. We go way back!"

Thinking it best to curtail the verbal tennis match between the ladies, Hollister interrupted, "Well, now that we've made introductions, would you like to join us for a drink, Jayne?"

Miss Blackwell declined the offer, excusing herself to rejoin her companion. "But I will hold you to our dinner date, Charles," she said. "And I do hope you haven't forgotten about our engagement tomorrow. We really must tend to that little matter we discussed, Darling."

Charles cast an uneasy glance at Marie. "To be honest, Jayne, that did slip my mind and I do need your input. See you then?"

"I wouldn't miss it for the world, Charles! We have *ever* so much to catch up on. Do contact me, Darling. I'm in suite 244. Shall we meet in your room or mine?"

He stammered, "Uh ... the la-lobby would be best."

"As you wish. I'll be there." Jayne kissed Hollister lightly on the cheek before nodding coolly at Marie. "Enjoy your meal." Marie appeared stricken as Miss Blackwell swung her curvaceous chassis toward the veranda.

Charles could read her mind. "A penny for your thoughts."

Marie looked up from her barely touched soufflé into Cary's twinkling eyes. "Keep your money; it's none of your business!" She paused to take another bite of fruit. "Miss Blackwell is pleasant and quite pretty, isn't she?" Marie waited for his reaction.

"Yes. Quite!"

Charles reached for Marie's hand, giving it a fatherly pat. "Well, Mimi, I have an appointment to get to, but I hope you have something terribly exciting to occupy yourself with this afternoon."

Appearing vexed, Marie drew her hand away, stood, and dabbed her lips on her linen napkin which she then tossed to the side of her plate. "Actually, I'm meeting a gentleman— a *close* friend. Sorry to rush off like this, but I need time to freshen up. Thank you for the lovely brunch. *Au revoir!*" Charles straightened his tie, making an irksome dig, "Well, give Bobby my best, and don't scrape your knees while tree climbing with the little dickens."

"I assure you, Mr. Hollister, the man I'm meeting is *not* Bobby." Marie turned, flouncing her fair curls, and departed with her own signature version of a sashay: *the Glide.* At the sound of his grunt, she turned her head enough to note his stunned expression, and smiled with satisfaction.

Passing through the main foyer of the hotel, Charles pondered the meeting between the two ladies. He could no longer deny his growing affection for Marie. Would she find his current feelings for her appalling? Did she see him merely as a friend, or have the sort of admiration a girl feels for an older brother or a favorite Uncle? *Is that what I am to her, as in how Bobby sees Marie?*

Then there was Jayne, who had suddenly reappeared in his life. She was more polished and attractive than ever, exuding refinement and sophistication. Her magnetic draw was hard to resist; on their sailing excursion, she'd proven to be an accomplished kisser.

He'd follow through with their dinner date. It would be common courtesy, at the very least. He'd keep his options open and take his sweet time before making a permanent commitment to anyone, if ever.

Hollister reached for a note card at the main desk, dipped the register's pen in the inkwell and wrote:

Dear Miss Blackwell,

This is to confirm our dinner engagement on Thursday evening in the Crown Room at 8:00 P.M. I'll also look forward to meeting you in the lobby tomorrow as planned.

Cordially, Charles B. Hollister, Room 396.

After neatly folding the note and slipping it into its small envelope, he addressed it in his manly scrawl, "Miss Jayne Blackwell, Suite 244." Handing the invitation to the desk manager, he requested it be delivered posthaste. He envisioned the evening would play out with the exchange of customary pleasantries; his relationships always tended to be stilted and orchestrated. The dozens of women he'd socialized with were lovely, cultured, and available, but not enough for him to take seriously. He'd made himself unobtainable … until now, perhaps. What had changed in his heart? And who was the man Marie was meeting?

Elsie answered the phone on the first jingle, hoping to hear Avery's voice on the other end of the line. She was not disappointed.

"Hello, Gorgeous! You're just the girl I want to talk to!"

His greeting gave her goosebumps. "Avery, how good of you to call!"

In a flirtatious tone, "You've been playing hard-to-get far too long regarding the screen test. There's an opening on the lot tomorrow morning, and I'm hoping we can fit you in. Please don't disappointment me this time; say you'll do it. Pretty please?"

Elsie jumped at the chance. "Well, it just so happens that Monday *is* my day off; tell me when and where, and I'll be there!" She could barely contain herself while hanging the receiver on its hook. Tomorrow might be her big break—the one that could change her life forever.

A glance at his watch reminded Bradley Smythe he was late for a crucial appointment. *Don't want to keep her waiting or she might give up on me.* He patted the lapel pocket of his light-weight summer sports coat, making sure the small box he'd tucked in there earlier had not slipped out. How would she receive what he had to say? *I hope her heart is in tune with mine, and she'll accept this token of my deepest and abiding affection.* He hadn't quite prepared himself for Coronado's breathtaking scenery. Yes, he'd bought up all the travel brochures he could get his hands on prior to boarding the train, but they didn't do the picturesque island justice. After inhaling body odors and stale cigars in a stuffy train coach for close to three full days, this was Heaven!

Thankful for the presence of mind to don a sunbonnet, Marie nervously paced the sun-drenched pier while waiting for Bradley to show up. Thinking about her feelings for him, she realized time apart from Brad had not made her heart grow fonder, after all. She was so like the unruly girl in her beloved Louisa May Alcott poem, whose "kingdom" was a mixture of longing to grow up and yearning to be a carefree child who threw caution to the wind. To be honest, she hadn't quite mastered the ability to take command of her willful temptations and naturally mischievous instincts, and doubted she was ready to settle down to a humdrum life. She mentally recited excerpts from *My Kingdom* while scanning the harbor for a glimpse of Bradley.

> A little kingdom I possess
> where thoughts and feelings dwell,
> And very hard I find the task
> Of governing it well;
> How can I learn to rule myself,
> to be the child I should,
> Honest and brave, nor ever tire
> Of trying to be good? ...
> Be thou my guide until I find
> Led by a tender hand,

Thy happy kingdom in myself
And dare to take command.

At last she spotted him waving his arm and jogging toward her. She'd wondered how it would feel after being apart for so long. Granted, she was glad to see him, but now she knew that beyond great admiration and fond friendship, she felt ... nothing. Up to this very moment, she hadn't allowed herself to make a final decision, but suddenly had her answer. She hated to hurt Bradley after all this time; he deserved someone who was over-the-moon in love with him. For herself, she knew she wouldn't be happy settling for a comfortable, broken-in shoe. No, she was saving her heart for a man she simply could not live without—a man who was exciting and unpredictable and would make her *tingle* every moment for the rest of her life. First and foremost was the music career she refused to abandon; a goal on which she and Bradley did not see eye-to-eye. *To thine own self be true.*

"You made it!" she greeted him. "Any trouble finding the place?"

He greeted her, a bit out of breath, "Sorry I'm late, Marie. Everyone around here seems to know about the Boathouse ... spotted the big sign a block away! Stopped to pick something up (patting a bulge in his coat pocket), and it took a little longer than expected. Gosh, you look good!"

Please don't let that be a ring! Marie hoped, as they embraced.

"You must be hungry and thirsty after your trip. How about if we order and then visit at one of the shaded tables?" she suggested.

"I definitely need to talk to you, Marie; to be honest, I'm too wound up to eat. Some cold water would hit the spot, but that's it." He loosened his neck tie. "Your August heat is pretty intense, even with the ocean breeze."

"True, but not as humid as Chicago." *Why are we talking about the weather?* "Okay," she agreed, "let's talk first." *Might as well get it over with quickly, like pulling off a Band-Aid*, she thought.

Bradley dropped into a chair, swept a chestnut wave from his sweaty forehead, and chugged down a glass of water before speaking his mind. "Marie, we've been an item for a long time, and talked about our future together, but we didn't make it official. I'm not sure why, exactly. I guess we both needed to grow up before making a permanent commitment." At this point, Bradley reached across the table and gently took Marie's hands in his own trembling ones. "I for one," he continued, "am now ready to make that kind of commitment." "Brad, *please* ... before you go on, let me say something!"

"Sorry, Marie, but it's now or never. You're so beautiful, intelligent, talented, and even funny—everything a man could want—and you could get any man you want. I'm honored you even give me the time of day. So, I need to come right out with it. Marie, will you be all right if that man ... *isn't* me?"

Marie felt like a fish with its mouth hanging open. "D-did I hear you correctly, Brad? Are you breaking up with me?"

Bradley's voice shook with emotion, "I'm afraid so, Baby, I finally realized that even though we're good friends and have had some wonderful times together, we're not right for each other. We each deserve God's best. I'd give anything not to hurt you. I do love you so very much, but not the way I used to think I did. It seems it was merely an adolescent crush, and we both deserve so much more."

Marie laughed hysterically with tears forming at the corners of her eyes!

"Please don't cry, Marie. I can't stand to see you cry!"

"These are not tears of sadness, but of total relief! You see, I realized this afternoon I'm not in love with *you*, either! Isn't it wonderful?! After all, Brad, we were never Elizabeth and Darcy," she giggled.

Puzzled, "Who?"

"Oh, it's a Jane Austen reference, meaning we won't be listed among the world's greatest lovers."

"And how! We're more like brother and sister." He grinned, deepening the cute dimples which had initially attracted her to him.

"But Brad ... you came all the way out here just to tell me that?"

"It's not kosher to break up with a girl long-distance, Marie. I'm too much of a gentleman to do that to you. Besides, I had some vacation time coming, and I've always wanted to see the West Coast. Plan to do some sightseeing."

"That makes me feel a little better," she said, "and I really am glad you came."

"Oh, I almost forgot!" Bradley reached into his pocket, pulled out a square, black velvet box, and handed it to her.

"What's this Brad? You shouldn't have!"

"If this conversation went as well as I hoped it would—which it did—I wanted to give you a token of our friendship. I had no idea what it should be. After I got off the bus, I spotted this in the jewelry shop window; it seemed perfect for you. That's what made me late getting here. Go ahead and open it!" Accentuated against the purple satin lining, nestled a beautiful gold violin brooch studded with a heart-shaped amethyst (her birthstone) that brilliantly sparkled in the sunlight.

Marie was deeply touched. "Oh Brad, it's beautiful, but far too much. I shouldn't accept such a lavish gift."

"Please keep it, Marie! It would mean so much to me if you would. Besides, I can afford it. Just got a big raise!"

Unable to resist, Marie consented. "To me, it will symbolize our heart strings, which can't be broken and will always be in tune. Is that too corny?"

Bradley grinned in agreement. "Yes, it's corny, but I was thinking along those lines, too, and didn't quite know how to say it. Here, let me pin it on for you." He leaned close to Marie, carefully fastening the glittering brooch to her bodice before kissing her on the cheek.

Charles Hollister needed time alone to sort out his conflicted feelings for the two catty women in his life. He'd taken a peaceful cruise around the bay, then docked his skerry before heading toward the Boathouse for fish and chips. Stepping onto the sun deck, he spotted a young couple. "What in the ... ?" Her face was partially blocked by a big, flowery hat, but no doubt about it ... there sat Marie with a fellow who looked very familiar. *Ah, yes! That pipsqueak, Smythe! Marie's old flame. What's he doing here?*

His heart sank at the sight of them holding hands, gazing into each other's eyes, and laughing like a couple of love-sick fools! To his horror, Charles watched as Smythe handed Marie a box containing a "sparkler," and leaned in for the kiss!

Unable to stomach any more of the disgusting scene, he turned on his heels and stormed back to his berth.

Right when I thought she was beginning to care for me, the little minx! Well, she's quite the deceptive actress, but no woman gets away with playing Charles Hollister for a fool! As far as he was concerned, they were all the same. "Use 'em and lose 'em" was their standard motto. *I finally let my guard down, and this is what I get!* Hollister angrily untied the Solitaire and sailed back out to sea.

Chapter Six

The persistent clackity-clack of a loose ceiling fan blade interrupted her dream ... at the very best part, of course! Precisely when sleep had finally claimed her heavy eye-lids, Elsie did not know; the chiming of the hall clock, every hour on the hour throughout the night, had made slumber as elusive as her fantasy reunion with Jack. It was a bit too early to crawl out of bed; the sun's rim had not yet peeked over the horizon. Relishing the coolest hours this late August day would offer, she pulled the sheet under her chin and listened to the mingled sounds of the annoying fan, a distant ship's horn, and the first screeches of seagulls in search of breakfast. She considered getting up to feed her own little fledglings, but the house was so quiet she chose not to disturb them. *Let them sleep.*

Elsie reviewed Avery's coaching tips, as she took advantage of her last moments of solitude. Perhaps this was the day when everything would change and she'd be on her way to a life which was tangible only to a select few. A new Hollywood director was in the early stages of shooting a western film at the cliff dwelling structure at Balboa Park—remnants of the 1915 Panama-California Exposition. The park was one of the most popular locations for production companies, since the natural scenic beauty and romantic architecture made it possible to film authentic outdoor scenes, eliminating the need and expense of building backdrops. San Diego's consistently pleasant weather made it possible to film outdoors year-round. According to Avery, her facial features, dark hair and eyes would be well-suited for the bit part of an Indian maiden. The rest could be taken care of with a little grease paint. Yes, it was a film "short," but he'd promised that America would fall in love with her. "The sky's the limit!" She was a lucky girl, and would be a fool to turn down this opportunity to make a name for herself.

Charles found himself automatically scanning the announcements section of the morning paper for news of Marie's upcoming nuptials. Perturbed with his own curiosity, he tossed *The Sun* in the lobby waste bin. Of course, it was too early for the banns to be posted. The sickening scene of the prior afternoon plagued him—replaying over and over in his head, making him feel like a horse's behind for even considering a serious relationship with a girl so young.

On the other hand, pursuing the mature, educated, and experienced Jayne Blackwell *did* make much more sense at the moment. A permanent merger with someone in her station of life would benefit both of them socially, professionally and financially. He enjoyed her company and did feel some affection for her, but love? Well, he'd learned the hard way on more than one occasion that love was overrated. Never again would he allow himself to be so gullible and vulnerable. He decided to let it all play out for now with Jayne, and see where it led.

And speaking of Jayne, she was due at any moment to accompany him on a buying venture downtown. He gritted his teeth, fearing it might end up costing him a pretty penny in more ways than one.

"Get in here and let me look at you! Well, aren't you cute?!" Mildred Gable chuckled while greeting her visitors. The O'Neill siblings hesitated, looking warily up at their mother for direction.

"It's okay kids. Mrs. Gable is going to take good care of you while I tend to some business this morning. You remember Mrs. Gable from church, don't you?"

Elsie's offspring silently nodded with frowns and pouts.

"Mommy, why can't we stay with Auntie Marie today, like always?" queried little Wilma with a trembling voice.

"Now Wilma, you know Marie has other plans today. I'll be gone for a few hours, and you'll have so much fun you won't even miss me!"

The children looked doubtful as they firmly grasped each other's hands (a rare occurrence) prior to cautiously crossing the threshold of Mrs. Gable's lavish abode. Once inside, they gazed in awe at their fascinating new surroundings. The home was furnished with many lovely antique pieces, family heirlooms and memorabilia, oriental rugs, classic books, and souvenirs of world travels. A love for art was made apparent by exquisite oil originals adorning the walls. The gay chirping of birds lilted through from the sunroom.

Mildred, a widow of 20 years and an advocate for the handicapped, believed in the value of every individual. She possessed a unique passion for those who were "differently-abled," and worked tirelessly to lead them out of the shadows of discrimination into the light of acceptance. She now spent most of her time within the walls of her two-story mossy green Victorian, which in her own words was maintained in its *quintessential* condition.

Mildred's open heart and home embraced any child in need of a comforting hug, a soft lap to cuddle in, or a fresh-squeezed glass of lemonade from her prized Meyer lemons. Known as "Grandma Millie" to many Coronado locals, she was loved by all and rarely lonely, thanks to her extended family. Her well-preserved beauty and warm and joyful spirit made her nearly impossible to resist.

After looking around, Bobby asked, "Do ya gots any toys ta play with?"

"Well, I have many wonderful story books, or we can sing fun songs together at the piano. And then, there's my birds!"

"Birds?" Wilma instantly perked up, curious.

"My yes! I have a great fondness for birds, and I own a sweet little pair of canaries. Hear them singing? I have also collected many figurines of various species. Each one has its own story. Would you like me to show them to you, now?"

The little ones nodded vigorously and allowed the stately Mrs. Gable to guide them toward the sunroom. Leaning on her cane, the eighty-year-old turned toward Elsie and mouthed, "They'll be fine!" Redirecting her attention to the children, "We'll have a jolly good time together!"

Marie practically floated along Orange Avenue on her way to a tea shop where she'd arranged to meet her friend, Suzanne Leach. She dreamily reviewed the previous day's rapid turn of events: the unwelcomed intrusion of the conceited Jayne Blackwell during brunch; the witty banter between herself and Cary; and then, being delightfully jilted by Brad! Somewhere in there she'd come to terms with her own heart, acknowledging her growing attraction for Charles Hollister. Yes, their age difference was a major issue, but one that could be surmounted. She was willing to try if he was. The biggest fly in the ointment was Jayne Blackwell, Cary's contemporary in every way. The reality of her own tender years and lack of experience sunk in. Marie had often wondered about the females Cary associated with, but they were merely figments of her imagination. This one was very real and very beautiful, and could spell trouble.

Should I spill the beans to Suz? What will she think if I tell her I might be falling for Cary now that Brad has set me free?

Marie's heart fluttered upon spotting him ahead—hat box in hand—exiting the millinery shop. She guessed he must be checking out the latest fall arrivals for her father's clothing establishment in Chicago. She smiled and raised her arm in an exuberant wave. "Bonjour, Cary!" Marie's greeting caught in her throat, for she had not expected Jayne Blackwell to emerge through the doorway on his heels. With a withering glance at Marie, Miss Blackwell possessively clutched Hollister's arm, and they strolled by with nothing more than cool, obligatory nods in her direction. She had definitely been snubbed! High-hatted, as her brother Frank would say!

I'd expect rudeness from her, but not from Cary! Sunday's parting scene at The Del instantly flashed before Marie's eyes, and she inwardly groaned with agonizing awareness and a sinking sensation. *What have I done?*

Marie's blue velvet eyes did not blink; the open journal, blank as her stare, sat next to a lukewarm cup of tea on the small round table. The clatter of china a few feet away lifted the fog, and she wondered how long she'd been daydreaming ... *and what's taking Suz so long?* They'd agreed to meet at Tea Thyme at two o'clock, and it was now nearly half past the hour. She focused her attention on the journal and recorded her daily entry:

> Fully unexpected,
> This stirring in my soul.
> Rearranged emotions
> Have spun out of control!
> Despite the confusion,
> I'm not sure that I would
> Be at all inclined to
> Stop it if I could.
> When these yearnings started,
> Remains a mystery.
> The seed and sprout of love,
> Too small for eyes to see.
> You have been my mentor,
> And guardian of my ways;
> Intervening capers
> With maddening forays.
> Just an old, "wet blanket"
> Who scorned my unkempt curls;
> But now, my thoughts of you
> Are not for little girls!
> Looking like a film star,
> You set my cheeks ablaze!
> Oh to feel my lips brush,

The contours of your face!
Would it be too brazen,
To hope for some small sign,
You'll forsake all others,
And faithfully be mine?

Mina had been watching her newest customer for several minutes. The young woman had finished writing in her notebook, so Mina refilled a tea pot and headed to the girl's table. "Would you like a warm up, Miss, and is everything all right?"

Looking up at the attractive middle-aged server, Marie replied, "Um, I'm fine for now, thank you. Waiting for a friend who highly recommends your specialty of the house, poppy seed coffee cake. It sounds simply divine."

"What a nice compliment! Please make yourself at home, and I hope your friend won't keep you waiting much longer. By the way, I'm Mina, owner and operator of this quaint little shop." Mina set down the hand-painted china pot before continuing. "Not to meddle, but you seem very distracted or sad. I saw the way you stared out the window earlier, apparently at nothing in particular. Is something troubling you, dear?"

"Nothing that can be fixed right now. I'm Marie, and it's nice to meet you. 'Quaint' is exactly how I'd describe this place. Your cozy Victorian decor makes me feel like I'm at Grandma's house."

"That's the ambiance I try to maintain." Mina glanced around for other customers who might be within earshot, then took the liberty of seating herself directly across from Marie. With a lowered voice, "But back to you. Since I spend many hours a day with the public, I've developed the ability to read their emotions by body language. The eyes, in particular, are tell-all. Of course we're total strangers, but sometimes talking to a neutral person feels safer than with a close friend or relative. So, if you ever need an objective set of ears, I'm here. When I'm not brewing tea, I'm in my little apartment upstairs. Feel free to call on me any time. I mean it." She paused while Marie appeared to fight a stream of emotion.

"My world does seem to be a bit upside-down today," Marie confessed, "but as my mother often says, 'This, too, shall pass.' I moved here from Chicago about five months ago, and it's all still a bit strange to me." Marie dabbed at a tear with her lace handkerchief.

Being able to relate to Marie's situation, Mina reached across the table and patted Marie's hand as she began sharing her own story. "Bless our mothers and their loving wisdom. Mine has passed on, but I often feel her presence when I'm troubled. When I was a little girl, I was lucky to have a doting Gramma who taught me her delicious Polish recipes ... no one could make kolaches like her! I dreamed of someday owning a tea shop where I could share Gramma's specialties every day of the week. After I emigrated from Poland to Chicago with my parents, I didn't lose sight of my dream. So, one day I headed west in pursuit of my life-long ambition. By the way, what a coincidence that we're both from The Windy City! I already feel a connection with you, Marie." Pausing to laugh at herself, "Oh my! I do ramble on, don't I?"

"I'm blessed to still have my wonderful parents," Marie replied, "but miss them terribly. My sister and I hope they can come to town for the holidays. Thank you for your gracious hospitality and kindness." She paused to control her shaky voice. "I need all the friends I can get, right now." Mina followed Marie's gaze toward the large, glass display case, and explained to her newest patron that it was filled with her grandmother's mouth-watering Polish pastries. Marie admitted to having a sweet tooth. "I'd love to sample all of your selections, so you might be seeing a lot of me!"

"I certainly hope so!" Mina's attention was drawn to movement outside the window. "She must be who you're waiting for—the one running across the street—am I right? She's been here before, like you said. I recognize her."

"Yes, at last!"

"I'll run back to the kitchen to warm up the coffee cake and make a fresh pot of tea."

A slightly disheveled, petite brunette raced into the shop and spotted Marie seated by the large picture window. She caught her breath, removed her business jacket, and smoothed the pleated skirt of her gray drop-waist jumper before being seated.

"Sorry I'm late, Kiddo. It was crazy at the studio this morning. I was supposed to get the whole day off, but they needed me for a few hours. The animators weren't satisfied with our painting on the celluloids, so we started all over, making cuts before getting *Alice* right. Walt is already the brunt of many jokes in Hollywood ... Laugh-O-Gram being referred to as 'Disney's Folly.' I believe in Walt, and consider it a great honor to be on his staff. We don't get paid much, but what I learn from the man is worth millions."

Drawing had always been Suzanne's favorite pastime, and she'd dreamed of being a professional artist. When she saw the job posting for Laugh-O-Gram in Kansas City, she jumped at the chance to apply and was hired on the spot. After the studio filed for bankruptcy, she and another painter, Lillian Bounds, followed Walt to the west coast to work on the *Alice Comedies*. Having created her own cartoon critters (squirrels, mice and lady bugs) as a child, Disney's characters had instantly found a home in Suzanne's heart. She'd been ecstatic when her school chum, Marie, moved to Southern California, and Suzanne drove down to Coronado as often as possible.

"No need to apologize for being late, Suz," Marie assured her friend. "I had a good conversation with the owner, so the time flew by. I'm famished, and looking forward to the coffee cake you raved about ... here it comes!" Just then, Mina emerged through the kitchen's swinging door, bearing a loaded serving tray.

Mina greeted Suzanne with a warm smile. "Good to see you again, and thanks for recommending me to your friend." She set the heavy tray on a nearby table before placing a dish of moist, warm cake in front of each lady. After pouring steaming cups of soothing chamomile tea from a hand-painted china pot, Mina set it on a hot pad in the middle of the table, and covered it with a quilted cozy.

The girls inhaled the scents of chamomile and cake while blowing across their piping-hot teacups. "*C'est si bon!*" Marie exclaimed with a look of ecstasy.

Mina beamed. "I took a little French in school, and am so glad you like my refreshments. *Merci beaucoup!* Enjoy, ladies, and don't be shy about asking for seconds. On the house!"

Suzanne savored her first buttery morsel while looking intently at Marie. "I know you love being nanny to your sister's kids, but what happened to your plan to enroll at the conservatory? Don't you want something more than pin money and a place to live? A fulfilling career and steady paycheck would be nice, wouldn't it?

Please don't give up on that dream. After all, no dream equals no dream come true."

Marie swallowed her mouthful and brushed a crumb from the bodice of her tailored, olive green sundress before answering. "Mmmm, this is delicious, or as Mama would say, 'nummy.' You're right, Suz. Wilma and Bobby will be starting school next week, and I *have* wondered how I could constructively fill those empty hours. So I've come up with a plan—the only one that makes sense to me right now. No, I'll never give up on my dream, and in the meantime, I'm going to teach violin lessons."

Suzanne expressed skepticism, "It sounds grueling. Are you sure you want to tackle it? I figured you might even try selling some of your poetry, or composing humorous memoires ... could be best sellers!"

"Hardly, Suz! The things I write about are far too personal to share with the world, but music is universal. When I was a kid, Pops made me practice my violin an hour every day, and I hated it! As you well know, one of The Academy requirements was music instruction, so I continued with what I already knew. I was pleasantly surprised that I enjoyed it so much ... mostly because Pops wasn't watching the clock in the next room. I get lost in music; it carries me away to exotic places, much like a good book does. Having you for a roommate was the best part. What fun we had with our violin-piano duets and little pranks we pulled on Mademoiselle Beaumont!" "Like running her corset up the flagpole!" Suzanne laughed so hard, she nearly choked on a crumb.

"Whose dumb idea was that, anyway? Yours or mine?" Marie asked with a broad grin.

"I don't remember, exactly, but Beaumont came down on us like a ton of bricks! Her blood was boiling! I thought she'd expel us for sure, Marie; but when we showed remorse and confessed our wicked deed, our penance turned out to be a month's worth of dish pan hands. We learned a whole new meaning to the term 'coming clean!'"

They reminisced about their crazy capers and giggled like school girls!

"She had a lot more gray hair by the time we graduated! We definitely were double-trouble, Suz, but I think Mademoiselle Beaumont actually had a soft spot in her heart for us. Good thing it wasn't a co-ed boarding school, or we'd have been kicked out, for sure!"

"No doubt about it! In my last annual she wrote the Shakespearean quote, 'To thine own self be true.'"

Marie nodded. "In mine, too! It may have been her way of saying that in spite of it all, she wouldn't change a single thing about our zany selves—urging us to follow our hearts and destinies, rather than conform to the expectations of others."

Suzanne switched subjects. "Honestly, Marie, are you sure you want to put yourself through the drudgery of listening to little prodigies squeak and squawk?"

"In spite of the hard work, I do think I'll enjoy it. I've missed my music these past months, since I left my violin in Chicago. I sent Pops a telegram last week asking him to ship it."

Suzanne was warming up to the idea, thinking it might work, after all. "What's the plan? Will you be teaching at an established studio?"

"That's a possibility for later on, but for starters, if I can work it around Wilma and Bobby's school schedule, I'd like to teach private lessons at home. Wilma shows an interest in everything I do, so it would be fun to teach her, too. She's at the right age to begin."

Suzanne drummed her fingers on the lace table cloth, as she considered the monetary factor. "You can't make much doing that."

"True, dear friend. You try to encourage me to be the best I can be, and I love you for it, but how much do you actually make at Disney? Music is my passion, like art is yours. If you think about it, most famous artists started with nothing."

"Point well taken, but I can see potential in people they don't usually recognize in themselves. I wish you only the best as you follow your heart and your dream. Hope it works out."

Suzanne studied Marie who had grown silent and was winding her strand of beads around her forefinger in an absent-minded manner.

Suzanne cut in, "You're off in your own little world, Marie. What's up?"

Marie sighed deeply. "Oh Suz, I don't quite know how to begin. Yesterday, what I want most was within reach ... or so I thought. That changed this afternoon. My heart is breaking, with no one to blame but myself." She told her everything, even confessing her realization of falling for Cary and that she hoped he cared for her, too. Marie tearfully ended with, "If only I hadn't said I was meeting another man. I sense he's hurt or angry with me and is moving on, weary of my immaturity and childish pranks. I'm so afraid I've lost my chance with him forever."

"That's pretty deep. However, you *do* realize Charles Hollister is old enough to be your father, don't you?"

Marie shook her head in rebuttal. "Not quite. More the age of an older brother."

"Well, you may be trying to convince yourself, but not me. You're young and beautiful and deserve to be with someone in your own generation who shares your zest for life and has the same

interests and experiences. I personally think it's hopeless to carry a torch for a man nearly twice your age. The older woman sounds like she's much better suited to him. Hollister's good looks and charm are attractive now, but what will happen in another twenty years when he's old and you're still in your prime? He won't be able to keep up with you, and everyone will think your kids are his grandchildren! Don't you think it will make a difference *then*?"

Marie choked on a sob, "All I know is I need at least a chance with him, Suz. Just one chance to find out if we're meant to be, before he gets away. Nothing else matters right now. This is killing me!"

"If he gets away, Marie, he isn't meant for you!"

Mina could not help overhearing part of the conversation.

The young ladies both lacked the experience and maturity needed to deal with such matters of the heart: dramatic Marie thinking it the end of the world; while sensible Suzanne seemed to dismiss Marie's affection for an older man—seeing it merely as puppy love. Mina offered a prayer of healing for her new friend's troubled spirits.

"Can we visit Gramma Millie again, Mommy, pleeease?!" Elsie was relieved her children had gotten on so famously with Mrs. Gable, who proved to be a wonderful childcare alternative. They loved her birds!

The screen test had been terrifying, yet fun. So many people fussing about made her feel like a real celebrity. Hair, makeup, posture, and lighting had to be exactly right for the perfect shots. She couldn't wait for the results, feeling confident and deliriously happy. She nearly pinched herself to ensure she wasn't having another one of her fantasy dreams. For the first time in her life, she was hobnobbing with rich, famous, and glamorous people! All because of Avery! She was on her way to being something more than just Jack's widow and Wilma and Bobby's mother. She'd be a *somebody*!

With his slicked back, dark hair and brilliant white teeth, Weston had smiled broadly throughout, appearing pleased. Elsie wanted to make him look good with his new discovery, so she strove to follow each direction given her to the letter. Afterward, Avery had begged her to spend the rest of the day with him, but she'd declined. Having been gone longer than anticipated, she envisioned her little ones anxiously awaiting her return. *My babies must come first!*

"I'll let you off the hook for now, Gorgeous," he'd said, "but next time, you're *all* mine!"

Chapter Seven

The Crown Room, Hotel Del Coronado

Jayne Blackwell liked what she saw reflected in a vertical window of the luxurious dining room: her own slinky image, dressed to the nines in a beaded cream-colored sheath with matching cap sleeve wrap.

She'd taken extra care to primp for this evening on her mission to capture the heart and soul of Charles Hollister. She'd suffered the torture of hot waving irons, the plucking of brows, the ticklish business of forming fingernails into a perfect moon manicure, and the finishing touch—a metal lip tracer for a flawless red cupid's bow.

She admired herself with smug satisfaction. Nothing had been left to chance. Charles was in the bag, and he'd forget all about that little tomboy he seemed so fond of. Yes, financial and professional conveniences drove her pursuit, but she could not deny the womanly longing she felt whenever he entered a room.

⚜

Hollister greeted Jayne with a kiss on the cheek and an approving smile before escorting her to their table. *WOW!! Gotta admit she's a looker—what some men would call a 'tomato.' And those gams! If I can get over my past failed relationships, we just might make a go of it.*

They engaged in small talk before getting down to the business of ordering. "Our leg of lamb is superb, Sir. Might I recommend it to you and your guest this evening?"

Charles's startled eyes met those of the dignified waiter. "Uh, no! Not tonight, Ignacio." (He'd had his fill of lamb lately, remembering a recent meal with another beautiful woman). "We'll start with the asparagus salad, and then the Alaskan King Crab."

"Excellent choice, sir. I'll bring your salads right out."

Jayne's asparagus remained untouched while looking intently at her date. She took a puff from her cigarette, and a curl of smoke mingled with her words, "I so enjoyed our shopping spree on Monday, Charles. I think we made some excellent choices for each of your associates, don't you? Would it be too presumptuous of me to say we make a good team?"

Hollister swallowed a bite of salad, along with a trickle of cigarette smoke. He lightly coughed and loosened his collar a bit; *Zowie, it's hot in here!* "Not presumptuous at all, Jayne. I think we work well together. You have excellent taste and a good eye for style and color. It's the artiste in you, and the reason you've made a name for yourself."

Jane reached up and fluffed the feather on her hair ornament. "I simply adore my new headband, Charles! You were such a dear to buy it for me."

"Don't mention it, Jayne. You earned it, since your advice will be invaluable to the business."

Jayne held his gaze with her mocha eyes, "Do you suppose there could possibly be something more *personal* to our relation-ship, not strictly pertaining to *business,* Darling?"

He tugged at his collar again, *These 20th Century females are forward! Give them the vote and they run amuck!* Clearing his throat with a dry cough, "Well, um, Jayne, you know I'm quite fond of you, and we do seem to have a strong chemistry; so maybe we should plan to spend more time together and see how it goes. Does that suit you?"

Miss Blackwell's scarlet Cupid's bow stretched into a dazzling smile. "It would be *ducky*, Darling! You know that I believe in striking while the iron was hot, so how about joining me at the Labor Day Beach Party? An afternoon under my *private* cabana sounds like the perfect place to start!"

Hollister couldn't deny being flattered by her open pur-suit, and inwardly chuckled, *She wasted no time! The woman has no shame!* The cabana might be a good idea, after all, he thought, since it would block his view of Marie and that twerp, Smythe, flapping around like a couple of love-sick gulls. "It's a date!"

Avery cornered Elsie at the end of her shift. "Alone at last! Got time for dinner while I give you the low-down on your screen test, Gorgeous?"

Elsie declined, "I'd love to say yes, but have to run home, check on my kids, and get to my second job at the diner. Can we make it another time, soon?"

With a boyish grin intended to make Elsie's pulse race, "That can be arranged. How about going with me to the Labor Day beach gathering? It will give the two of us all day to relax and discuss every detail!"

Elsie instantly accepted that invitation. "Swell! Wilma and Bobby *love* the beach, and we rarely have an entire day to spend together. I can pack a picnic lunch and ask some of the gang from Callahan's to join us for a weenie roast!"

His smile faded. *What does she not understand about the 'two of us'?* He hadn't spent much time around kids, and wasn't too interested in starting now. He responded to Elsie, with waning enthusiasm, "Yeah, *SWELL* ... I'll see you *all* there."

Weston gazed with longing at her departing figure as she left the lobby. He'd have to work harder to bend her towards a more broad-minded, modern way of thinking.

September 1, 1924

All of Coronado would celebrate Labor Day by splashing and playing along the shore, stuffing themselves with hot dogs, listening to jazz bands, and having a razzle-dazzle good time as they oohed and aahed during the grand finale: a spectacular fireworks display over Glorietta Bay. Yes, all of Coronado, except Marie. This had been the worst week of her life. Any attempts she'd made to clear the air with Cary were to no avail: messages had been ignored, and there'd been no sign of him around town. All she actually knew from Elsie was that he'd been seen a time or two with Jayne Blackwell. Engulfed in a sense of overwhelming loss, Marie reminded herself that you can't lose what isn't yours to begin with. Nonetheless, her heart was breaking. She prayed that Cary's guardian angel would protect and guide *his* heart.

Little Wilma, sporting a green and white ruffled swim costume and bright pink sand pail, had begged her to go with them. "Sorry, Willie, but I'm not feeling well today. Run along and have fun, and you can tell me all about it when you get home," was her excuse to the disappointed little redhead. Elsie, taking one look at her sister, asked no questions.

Not having the stomach to witness Cary strutting his tanned, muscular physique with Miss Blackwell hanging all over him, Marie opted to stay behind in the seclusion of her bedroom. Second only to her faith in God, was the trust and comfort she found in writing. She plumped pillows behind her back and sat cross-legged on her bed, journal on her lap, as she allowed the emotions of her troubled spirit to flow with the ink:

> Sometimes the day seems twice as long,
> Worries loom over like giants,
> Body and spirit groan with fatigue,
> My heart aches for unfulfilled dreams.
> When I'm sure I can stand no more,
> And wonder why it is you tarry,
> I close my burning eyes and listen;
> But not to earthly surroundings.
> My ears search for an echo of sound
> From that higher plane where *you* are.

Unable to finish, she closed the book and wept.

Avery Weston lounged on the beach blanket, waiting for Elsie who was talking to her mixed assortment of "foreign" friends a few yards away

"Hey, Mister! Ya wanna help us build a sand castle?!" Bobby ran up to him, flinging sand from his blue bucket. Enraged, Weston sprang to his feet, brushed himself off, and grabbed at Bobby's hair.

"Whoa, there fella! Keep your meat hooks off the kid!"

Startled, Avery turned to see Stanley Harrison holding the leash of a magnificent golden retriever. Covering, Weston smiled stiffly and patted Bobby's hair (instead of yanking it). "Sorry, Buddy, I'm not much good at that sort of thing. Run along, now."

He turned towards Stanley with a challenging stance, "What's your beef? The little guy and I were having a private conversation, so keep your snoot out of our business! I'm practically his Daddy, so I have the right to do as I please!"

Stanley did not back down. "I've been watching you, and I don't like what I see. If I ever even *think* you aren't treating Mrs. O'Neill or her children right, you'll have *me* to answer to!"

Weston sized up his rather scrawny adversary, with the term milquetoast coming to mind. "My, my! I'm so scared! Let's see how brave you are when you don't have your body guard attached to you!"

The dog's snarling wiped the cocky smirk off Weston's face, and he retreated with a warning. "Make sure you keep your vicious mutt on its leash, or you might end up in stir!"

Holding his gaze on Weston, Stanley patted his faithful, agitated friend, "Simmer down, Becket. Good boy!" Heading toward the shoreline, he called out to Bobby, "I'll help you with your castle, son!"

Farther down the beach, Charles Hollister sipped a Prohibition Sour in the shade of Miss Blackwell's red-and-white-striped cabana. Unable to help himself, his eyes kept searching the coastline for a glimpse of Marie. Jayne inched closer to him, lightly brushing her fingertips along his bare forearm. "It's like we're in our own little world—just the two of us on a desert island. Isn't it romantic?"

He leaned towards her slightly-parted lips as her strong, spicy Bois perfume wafted through his sinus passages and tickled his throat. To avoid coughing in her face, he suddenly stood up, and vigorously stretched his muscular arms and shoulders. "I've been sitting here far too long. Going for a dip! Want to join me, Jayne?"

Jayne shrieked, "What?! Ruin this expensive coiffure?!"

Hollister bounded away, deeply inhaling the fresh air. "Well, suit yourself, then," thinking how Marie would have yelled *'last one in's a rotten egg,'* and plunged head-first! Where was she, anyway? Surely, not already on her honeymoon?! That would be too impetuous, even for her! Wading through breakers, he muttered, "I need to get her out of my head, but how? There's only one person I can turn to."

"Auntie Madge, is that you?!"

Margaret Middleton was having the time of her life under a large cabana with a group of stylish, middle-aged women. The ever-popular Madge had become quite the Hollywood socialite, following the end of a disappointing marriage to a "rounder," as she called him. She heard someone call her name, and caught sight of her eldest niece, Elsie O'Neill.

"Hallelujah, it's Elsie! How did you spot me?"

"I'd know you anywhere, Auntie, especially by your infectious laughter!" Elsie wrapped her arms around her father's flamboyant sister, giving her a squeeze.

"I hoped to run into you down here, Elsie! A sight for sore eyes! And the kiddies have grown like weeds!" Madge lifted the brim of her flowered garden hat while peering curiously at the man standing next to her niece. "How about introducing me to your friend?"

Elsie giggled, "Sorry! I'm so surprised to see you, I forgot my manners. Auntie Madge, please meet my new friend, Avery Weston. Avery, this is my aunt, Margaret Middleton."

Madge warily extended her hand to Avery. "Weston, hmmm ... rings a bell, but I can't quite place you."

Avery accepted her handshake with a loose grip, looking uncomfortable. "A pleasure to meet you ma'am." Then, turning abruptly toward Elsie, "I hate to break up this reunion, but shouldn't you be getting the little ones home? They start school in the morning, don't they?"

"He's right, Auntie, but please stop by and see us while you're in town. We're in a small bungalow." She pulled a note card from her bag and scribbled down the address. "It's the gray one with white trim and a red door. Can't miss it. Marie will be thrilled to know you're in Coronado."

Still squinting at Weston, she inquired of her niece, "By the way, where *is* Marie?"

"She didn't feel well today, Auntie, but I'm confident you're exactly what she needs. You have a knack for making her laugh, which she hasn't done much of lately."

"There's a story here you're not telling me. What's the best time?"

"Just about any time. I'm working two jobs, but Marie sticks close to the house for Wilma and Bobby. Since they're starting school this week, she'll welcome a nice visit ... just the two of you."

"Tell her I'll be there at eight o'clock in the morning, sharp ... and to put on a big pot of coffee ... *strong*, Okay?" Then, taking a drag on her long cigarette, she examined Weston like an unidentified germ under a microscope. "I know I've seen you somewhere. It will come to me."

Bloodshot and swollen. She surveyed the damage from yesterday's deluge of tears and frantically splashed cold water over her raw, puffy eyelids. *No use! There's no way to hide this from Auntie Madge!* Marie steeled herself for the forthcoming interrogation, but talking about it might actually help. Her tender-hearted and perceptive aunt had been a good sounding board and source of wisdom in the past.

Saying good-bye to the children didn't help matters. They were terrified at starting school in a new place with strange faces. Poor little Bobby was entering Kindergarten and had no idea what school even was. She used her soggy handkerchief to dab at a stream trickling down her cheek, amazed to have any moisture left at all.

Wilma and Bobby clung to her skirt, begging to stay home with Auntie Marie; but Elsie firmly, yet gently, pried them loose and nudged her whimpering children out the door ... nearly crashing into Margaret Middleton!

Madge swept into the house, jingling flashy charms. After taking one look at Marie, she chortled, "I didn't know the circus was in town!"

"Whaaat?"

Madge laughed heartily. "That big red nose looks like you're ready for a clown audition!"

Marie self-consciously placed her fingers over her nose, and managed to snicker. "I *am* a sight, aren't I?"

"At least I got you to crack a smile. You know what they say: laughter is good for the soul, *and* for a troubled heart." She paused to fill her nostrils with the rich aromatic scent emanating from the kitchen, "Mmm, mmm! I smell coffee! Lead me to it, and we'll hash this mess out ... whatever it is!"

Marie spent the remainder of the morning updating her aunt on the latest developments in her love life (what little there was of it). Hearing her own words, the story sounded a bit silly in light of Madge's even sadder story of love gone wrong. Nonetheless, Madge gave Marie her undivided attention until Marie had finished sharing her story.

"Auntie, this must sound so trivial to you."

With a wave of bejeweled hands, "Nonsense!" she exclaimed. "When has a broken heart ever been trivial? If we don't hurt once in a while, we're not really alive. Like they say, it's better to endure the pain of love lost than never to have loved at all!" Her bracelets jingled to the rhythm of her animated exclamation.

"True, but I keep thinking about you ..."

Madge interrupted with sadness clouding her eyes. "That's history, honeybun; but it did take me awhile to get over Harvey. I believe he loved me as much as he was capable of loving anyone, but his insatiable thirst for boot-leg whiskey and flappers did him in. I couldn't compete. When he asked me to bail him out of the clink after his third speakeasy raid arrest, I knew it was over." Madge wrapped her fingers around the coffee mug and took a sip before continuing. "On the bright side, I'm content to remain single and try to live life to its fullest in my own carefree, unencumbered way. Life's too short to endure betrayal and rejection. I wish Harvey the best, but the last I heard, he hadn't changed. Each of us must live with the consequences of our own choices."

"If only I knew what my choices were regarding Charles Hollister. He's avoiding me, and there's nothing I can do about it."

"Well, for Heaven's sake! Why don't you just march over to that hotel and have it out with him? It seems like the most direct approach to me."

"Direct, is right, Auntie. But doesn't that seem too forward or desperate? He hasn't answered any of my messages. I've grown out of my unrefined ways, and am not about to throw myself at him! The ball is in his court."

With a misty wink, Madge reached across the table and gently placed her hand over Marie's. "I see your point. While you're waiting for Hollister to make the next move, give it to God and trust in His timing. Let's pray about this together, shall we?"

After the "amen," they lifted their heads and smiled into each other's eyes. "I feel so much better, Auntie Madge.

Thanks for coming and listening to my tale of woe." Madge gave her niece a hug and stated, "I need to have a little chat like this with your sister, too, while I'm in town. The sooner the better! If that Weston character turns out to be who I think he is, he's up to no good!"

Wilma and Bobby chattered like a pair of magpies, trying to one-up each other with stories of their exciting day at school. They could hardly wait for Day Two (what their mother and aunt had hoped for).

On Wednesday morning, a more light-hearted Marie dropped them off at the school house and headed downtown. Nearing a corner, her heart nearly leapt out of her chest. There was Cary, with travel clothes and valise, stepping onto a streetcar. "Cary, wait!" she yelled.

Charles jerked his head in her direction, and nodded gravely before vanishing inside the car. With a clang and metallic squealing of rails, he was gone.

Chapter Eight

Downtown Coronado

Bessie Smith crooned her soulful *Down Hearted Blues* through the Radiola speakers as Marie approached the *Eagle's* classifieds desk. Still shaken from Cary's unmistakable rebuff moments earlier, she struggled to collect her thoughts before getting down to business, and wondered if her own blues would forever be with her. Marie stated her concise add to the clerk: "Violin Instruction: Beginner, Intermediate and Advanced levels. $0.50/hour. Call M. Middleton, CO-1090, Coronado, California."

Perhaps keeping busy and doing what she truly loved would lift the cloud of gloom, bringing joy and purpose to life. For now, nothing could erase the image of Cary's dismal expression as he boarded the streetcar. She wished with all her heart that he'd waited a moment and given her chance to clear the air. *Where is he going and for how long?*

"It's, Marie, right?"

Startled by a familiar voice, she spun around, coming face-to-face with the amiable owner of Tea Thyme. "Mina! How nice to see you, again! What brings you here?"

"I was about to ask you the same thing. I'm placing the ad for my autumn special, Caramel Apple Muffins. Not Gramma's recipe, but a favorite among my clientele."

"They sound fabulous, Mina! I can't wait to try one!"

Mina said she liked Marie's idea to solicit violin students, and assured her of the many music lovers in Coronado who might be interested. Mina promised to refer some of her acquaintances.

Changing the subject, Mina asked, "How have you been since our last talk? You seemed rather down in the mouth."

Marie's slumped shoulders and crestfallen expression spoke volumes. "Oh, not so good. Everything's the same—or worse—and there's nothing I can do about it. I've talked to those closest to me, and each person offers slightly different advice. I remember what you said about talking to a neutral person. I'm wondering ..."

"You don't even have to ask!" Mina broke in.

They arranged to meet at Tea Thyme the following day to chat over some of those featured muffins. Sharing such private emotions with a near stranger seemed awkward, yet the anticipation of opening up to her new friend gave Marie hope.

"I'm at my wits end. God bless you, Mina. I'll see you then!"

September 10, 1924

Dear All,

This is the first moment I've had to answer your letter. Such a busy time of year! Pardonnez-moi, s'il vous plaît (please forgive me).

You'd be very proud of your little sister, Martha. She's growing up so fast and is a good companion for me. Your father enrolled her in voice lessons, and she sings like a canary at all hours of the day and night! Frank loves to tease and his baby sister and calls her a "mocking bird!" Dear old Isabella and our new Cocker Spaniel, Sibbie, express their opinions by howling! Your father swears Martha will one day be a famous vocalist, but *je ne sais pas* (I don't know). As for your brother, he seems to be in a serious relationship, at last! We have not met his young lady, but anyone who Frank would choose has to be *merveilleux*! You know about his passion for aviation and barnstorming. Well, it seems he met this girl last spring at the Checkerboard Airdrome during a stunt show. Believe it or not, she's a wing walker! *Ça alors* (how about that)!

Which leads me to the most difficile part of my letter. As much as we long to see you, we simply cannot get away for the holidays. Martha will be a soloist in the school Christmas choir, and Frank wants us to meet his sweetheart, Connie Tanner, on Christmas Eve. She's on a cross-country tour until then. We expect them to make an announcement, since he writes to her every day and has never looked happier.

En j'en passe (and that's not all), you know how busy your father's company is during the holidays and how he thinks the place can't run without him there. However, we had a long talk about this and will look forward to spending Christmas with you, the sunshine, and palm trees next year!

As you must know, Charles Hollister is here indefinitely on business. He and Hugh are hard at work putting together the winter and spring lines. Charles brought many good fashion leads from his other associates out west. He alluded to a personal matter, as well. I'm concerned about him. He's not his usual confident self; he seems distracted and even *triste* (sad). I pray for him every night, as I do for you, chéries.

I love and miss you so! Give *mon petits enfants* (grandchildren) a kiss!

A bientôt (until later), Mama

Marie groaned as she folded the letter and placed it in her lap. *A whole year! But now at least I know where Cary is;* it didn't sound like he'd be back any time soon. What could the personal matter be? Hopefully, nothing to do with snooty Jayne Blackwell!

Home again—the only real home he'd known since he was five years old. Charles Hollister stood in front of the three-story, eighty-year-old edifice, and fought a flood of emotion. Orphanage of the Holy Infant in Oak Park, Illinois, was more than mortar and brick. It was a living, breathing refuge for the abused, neglected, or abandoned. More than fifty-percent of the children who passed through its doors had at least one living parent, as had been his case: parents in crises who needed safe lodging for their offspring. For the first time in weeks, he began to feel hopeful, knowing that the answers to his questions and Sister Faith awaited within the walls of Holy Infant.

The few days he'd spent in the city had revealed nothing of Marie's engagement. Hugh Middleton had made no mention of it, nor had he found the announcement in San Diego area or Chicago newspapers. Strange, yet he'd lacked the nerve to bring it up. Not that it should matter. Whatever their relationship had been (fun while it lasted), the time had come for both of them to move on. Coming home would give him the courage to head in that direction. Oh, how he hoped it was so!

Little Arnold Wilcox's rendition of what he called "The Alley Cat Waltz," did indeed sound like cats, but more like a cat *fight* than a waltz! His teacher made a mental note to pick up a set of earplugs the next time she went to town.

"Isn't he marvelous, Miss Middleton?!" cooed Mrs. Wilcox. "A genuine child prodigy! He taught himself to play this piece."

Marie made an attempt at diplomacy, "Um, I can see that." She pulled a copy of *Ševčik School of Bowing Technic for the Violin* from her music collection, and placed it on the stand in front of the alleged little genius. "For starters, Arnold, we need to review the basics and warm up with rhythmic exercises."

Arnold spotted a nearby candy dish and stuffed his mouth with spearmint leaves. His mother seemed distressed, but not with her little wonder. "Oh my! Exercises? Nothing too strenuous, please. He's a delicate child, so we must not run the risk of injury." Arnold turned a cartwheel across the braided parlor rug, ending in a handstand.

Marie struggled to suppress a giggle. "Not the type of exercise you might have in mind, Mrs. Wilcox. We're going to use some simple bowing methods which will strengthen Arnold's tone and technique."

Mrs. Wilcox sounded skeptical, "Well, please bear in mind that my Arnie is a future candidate for Julliard in Manhattan!"

"Hmmm, Manhattan ... sounds like a good place for him!"

Callahan's waitresses busied themselves clearing and resetting tables prior to the dinner crowd. Mitzi blurted out, "Okay Chica, let's have it! I can't wait any longer! What did Señor Weston say about the screen test? I saw the two of you with your heads together at the beach. If you're leaving me for Hollywood, I'd rather know now than later!"

Elsie laughed while filling a napkin holder, "Mitzi, you slay me! Let's not jump the gun. I'm not going anywhere, at least for a while. The producer told Avery that even though the camera likes me, I need a little more time to learn the ropes of the business. I'm thinking about getting my hair bobbed to look more stylish and sophisticated. Maybe that will make a difference."

Mitzie knew she was being selfish, but was very happy to hear that Elsie wasn't leaving any time soon. She asked what it would take to be good enough for a part.

"Avery thinks I need to spend a lot of time around those in the industry to pick up pointers," Elsie replied. "He wants to take me to a club where he says the crème de la crème gather."

"A club, Elsie? You don't mean a *speakeasy*, do you? *¡Aye-yai-yai! ¿Estás loca?! ¡Esas son malas* (Are you crazy?! Those are bad), and get raided all the time! Don't you read the newspaper?! If Paddy finds out, he'll give you the axe!"

"You slay me, Mitzie!" Elsie assured her dramatic friend that Avery wouldn't place her in danger; the clubs were well hidden from the authorities and other intruders, she added. "It takes a secret code to get in, Avery says, and it's well guarded. Besides, it sounds exciting, and it's time for me to have some fun and live for a change."

Mitzi crossed herself and looked toward the ceiling, praying aloud, "*¡Ay no!* Lead us not into temptation, but deliver us from evil!"

Mina was a good listener with a gift for knowing what made people tick. After hearing the whole story from Marie, Mina surmised the problem lay more with Charles. "I'm guessing something in his past prevents him from fully committing his heart. It may never be resolved; but I hope for his sake, and for yours, he comes to terms with it soon."

Marie said it wasn't an angle she'd considered. "I thought all this time that I simply wasn't enough woman for him. It's not much to go on, but better than nothing at all."

Madge Middleton swept into Callahan's, dramatically waving a feathery fan, and plopped into a booth. "Elsie Josephine, we need to talk!"

"Why, good morning to you, *too*, Aunt Madge!" Elsie greeted her with an amused expression. "Is something wrong?"

Her agitated aunt's voice elevated as she spoke. "Something *will* be wrong if you don't heed my advice! How much do you know about this Weston character you've been parading around town with?"

Elsie glanced around the diner, and motioned to her aunt to lower her voice. "Avery? Oh, he's simply wonderful, Auntie. He's been so good for me and treats me like a queen!"

"Well, I know of a man with a similar name who looks a lot like your boyfriend—except with lighter hair—and has quite a reputation in Hollywood for treating *many* naive young women like queens. He gives them *all* the royal treatment—Henry the Eighth style! (She made a slashing motion across her throat with her index finger). Let's hope he's not the same person!"

Elsie looked stunned and turned defensive, "Madge Middleton! You certainly can't be talking about the man *I* know! You're grossly mistaken, and how dare you insinuate he's a murderer?! What proof do you have? I also resent your implication that I'm *naive*!"

Madge took a cleansing breath to calm her jangled nerves before clarifying herself. "The man I'm talking about is not a murderer, exactly, but there've been more than a few would-be starlets who *wished* they were dead! Don't say I didn't warn you, honeybun, and don't be so enchanted by his smooth-talking spell you lose your head!"

"Arnold, come down this instant! Your mother will be back soon and mustn't find you dead!" Marie looked upward, shading her eyes from the bright afternoon sun with her hand.

Arnold's lips were moving in a muffled response. Unable to make out the words, it dawned on her. Of course! She pulled the wax plugs from her ears and raised her voice in response, "What did you say, Arnold? Watch out! You're going to fall!"

Curly-top "Arnie," performing a death-defying balancing act, contradicted with a cocky response. "Malarkey! I climb on roofs all the time. I'm a mountain goat! Never fall ... not even once!"

A strange, male voice behind her called out, "Hey, pal! Don't let this be your *first* time!" Marie spun around and met the gaze of an exceptionally handsome young man, whom she guessed to be her new pupil. "Need some help with the kid?" he asked with a charming smile.

"Uh, no, I guess not. He's coming down on his own." Feeling a little weak in the knees, Marie composed herself and extended her hand, "I'm Marie Middleton. I assume you are ..."

He finished her sentence, "Woods. Jonathan Woods," then shook her hand, and grinned. "Pleased to meet you Miss. I was expecting an older person, not someone like *you*!"

With both feet on solid ground, Arnold interrupted the awkward moment with, "When I grow up, I wanna be a builder. Then I can climb on stuff all day!"

"Or be in the circus!" Jonathan laughed heartily.

"Yoo-hoo! Arnie! Mother's here!" Mrs. Wilcox slammed the driver's side door of her black Model T.

"Oh goody," Arnold mumbled to his flabbergasted teacher.

Inside the house, Arnold's mother picked up his violin case while Marie stated her misgivings regarding the boy's future as a musician. "Mrs. Wilcox, as fond as I am of Arnold, I must be honest and say this isn't working out."

Arnold's mother brushed past her, glaring over her tortoise-shell spectacle frames on her way to the front door. "Whatever do you mean, Miss Middleton? Exactly *what's* not working out and for *whom*?"

"Well, Arnold is easily distracted and we don't seem to accomplish much during his lesson time. I know it's your dream for him to be a virtuoso, but I sense he has his sights set on something ... *higher*."

Woods had been eavesdropping from the porch and hid a snorting sound behind his straw Panama hat. Marie bit her bottom lip to suppress a laugh.

"Higher?!" Mrs. Wilcox shrieked. "What's higher than *Julliard?!*"

"I'm sure you want what's best for Arnold, don't you?"

"Miss Middleton! I certainly *do* know what's best for my own son!" Mrs. Wilcox grabbed her juvenile delinquent's hand, and indignantly strutted outside with a pointed, "Don't worry, Arnie. Mother will find you a *new* teacher. The last *three* have proven to be *incompetent!*" The porch steps creaked beneath her ample mass as Mrs. Wilcox tromped from the premises.

The little dickens turned his head toward Marie with an impish wink and grin, "See ya later, Doll!"

Jonathan Woods guffawed right out loud! "You must've had your hands full with *that* kid!"

"Actually," Marie replied while wiggling her fingers at the departing Wilcoxes, "I think I'm going to miss the little monster. It seems the two of us have a lot in common! "But we're cutting into your lesson time. You said you haven't played since high school, right?"

Jonathan followed her into the house. "Yeah, seven years ago, but I was pretty good then, if I may say so. Life got in the way, and there's been no time to practice; I *would* like to get back to it—mostly for my own enjoyment."

"Let's start by determining what level you're on now. Did you bring any familiar music with you?"

Woods laid his briefcase on the sofa and opened it. "As a matter of fact, I did. I picked out one of the easier ones so I wouldn't make too big a fool of myself right off the bat." He handed her a somewhat dog-eared copy of *Vivaldi-Nachèz Concerto in A Minor.*

"One of my favorites, but easy only to an accomplished musician. Most of my students start out with *Mary Had a Little Lamb!*" she tittered.

Jonathan tightened and rosined the bow before tuning his instrument. "Okay, here goes nothing!" Setting the chin rest comfortably in place, he lightly pulled the bow across the strings, gradually increasing with confidence and intensity. He completed the concerto with sweat pouring from his brow and silently waited for Marie's analysis.

"Mr. Woods, I'm speechless! For someone who hasn't played in years, it was impressive. Yes, a little rough, but with daily practice and weekly lessons, you'll soon have it mastered and move on to more advanced pieces. You show great potential."

His eyes held hers with a relieved gaze for a moment, before his mouth twisted into a flirtatious grin. "I like that word ... *potential!* Do you suppose there's any potential of us having a bite to eat together sometime?"

Marie flushed at the suggestion. "Mr. Woods! I don't think it would be appropriate. I'm your *teacher*, for crying out loud!"

"Aw, come on, Miss Middleton. It's the 20th Century!"

Marie could not resist the challenge and gave in. "Well, I suppose it would be okay ... as long as we discuss *music*."

"How about dinner on Friday, *Teacher?*"

She returned his exuberant smile and thought, *maybe getting out will shake off my downhearted blues.* "It's a date!"

Chapter Nine

Early October, 1924

"Be careful ..."

The ominous warning echoed through inky darkness, growing fainter and fainter along with his image. The other times he'd laughed, joked around, and called her his Jo Jo. She'd open her eyes with sweet kisses lingering on her lips, feeling warm and comforted. Tonight he'd left her with the heebie-jeebies; hearing those two words over and over ... his foreboding expression was imprinted on her memory. "Jack? Oh Jack! What are you trying to tell me?"

With an icy chill traveling down her spine, she sat up and lit the bedside lamp. She looked around her bedroom and found nothing amiss. She was alone, yet he'd been right here seconds ago. Hadn't he? It had been so real, yet logic told her it was only a dream.

Too on edge to sleep, she shoved her feet into pink satin boudoir slippers and shuffled her way to the kitchen. *Warm milk usually does the trick. I'll try that.* She set a saucepan on the burner, and she racked her brain for a clue to the meaning of Jack's message while the milk heated.

Then, Auntie Madge's own warning rang in her ears, making
her shiver all over again, "there've been more than a few would-be
starlets who *wished* they were dead! Don't say I didn't warn you ..."

Charles rubbed the sleep from his eyes upon waking from
the most satisfying rest he'd enjoyed in ages, in his very own familiar bed (at least the only bed he truly considered his own).
What a luxury it was to come home to the room Sister Faith
made sure was ever ready and waiting for him—as though he'd
never left. He'd arrived well after dark the night before, so had
tiptoed past the rooms where the other inhabitants soundly slept
and headed straight for bed. Sister Faith had promised a leisurely
brunch and heart-to-heart after her morning dormitory rounds.
However, his first order of business was to greet Sister Agnes. Now
over 80, the officially retired Mother Superior continued to fill a role at
the orphanage as a dear family member, spiritual mentor, and prayer
warrior. Charles found her in the nursery where she gently cradled a
colicky baby in need of her magic touch. Her rheumy, gray eyes pooled
with tears at the sight of him. Charles bent over the elderly woman
and the infant with a tender hug and planted a kiss atop her wimple.
"Glory be! You've come home, my son! Oh how I prayed I'd see you
again. At my age, anything can happen."

"Don't be so melodramatic, Mother! You haven't aged a
day since I saw you," Charles admonished, playfully shaking his
index finger. "I *expect* you to be around for a *long* time to come!"
Seeing her precious face again made him realize how much he'd
missed her. "It's so good to be home! In the business world, years fly

by like weeks. Sadly, what's closest to one's heart can unintentionally get lost in the shuffle."

Sister Agnes carefully laid soundly sleeping Preston in his crib and turned to Charles. "I need some fresh air, so how about taking an old woman for a walk this beautiful October morning?"

"You took the words right of my mouth!" Charles tenderly cradled her arm as he slowly strolled alongside the woman he'd come to think of as his own mother, leading her to the courtyard.

"I love Midwest Autumn with its changing colors and brisk air. I remember how much fun Jack and I had romping through piles of fallen leaves."

Sister Agnes chuckled. "I'd send you boys outside to rake them up, and you'd end up *wearing* most of them!"

Charles grinned, remembering. "Hard to avoid, the way we rolled around! I still love the pungent scent of dried maple leaves and how they crackle underfoot. Such a glorious time of year!" "You may remember Sister Eymard collecting and pressing the beautiful autumn leaves. She still does that, and is teaching the children to dip them in paraffin to preserve their colors longer." "Yes, Mother. I do remember her teaching us how to do that. It's tricky business; once Jack accidentally spilled the pot of hot wax. No one was burned, but it was an awful mess to scrape up!"

A cloud seemed to pass over Agnes as they reminisced. "It broke my heart to learn of Jack's passing. I loved him like my own, but it's such a comfort to know he's safe with God and that we'll see him again one day."

Charles nodded. He didn't have any close friends until Jack and Margaret Kathleen (now Sister Faith) came to Holy Infant after the tragic death of their parents. Even though Jack was five years younger than Charles, they hit it off and quickly became as close as brothers. "I felt his loss keenly, but it's been much harder on Elsie. However, it looks like she might be ready to move on with her life."

Sister Agnes nodded. "Life does go on, even when we think it won't. God has a plan and season for everything He sends our way, whether it be joy or sorrow. He makes all things work together for good when we put our trust in Him."

Soft steps on the pavement and a rustle of skirts drew their attention to Sister Faith and Sister Eymard who had followed them at a discreet distance. "Sorry to interrupt," said Sister Faith, "but we've finished our rounds, and I wondered if you were ready for that visit, Chuck. We can make it later if you need more time."

"I'd love to spend the entire day with this handsome fellow," Agnes interjected, "but I'm feeling a little worn out. If you'll be so kind as to take me to my room, Charles, I'll let Faith have you all to herself ... but only for a *little* while," she added with an impish smirk.

Love exuded from Sister Faith's eyes as she smiled at the elderly woman. "I'll be waiting for you in the dining room, Chuck, whenever you're ready."

Sister Eymard gave Charles a warm hug. "It's wonderful to see you, dear Charles. It's been too long! I'll prepare some breakfast for you and Faith to enjoy during your private visit, and you and I will catch up a bit later."

Sister Eymard made his homecoming complete. She first came to the Orphanage of the Holy Infant at the age of 14 as a young novice ready to devote her life to serving God.

Charles swallowed a lump in his throat, remembering that she was the one who taught him his first prayers in Catechism so long ago. He noticed how she'd aged but hadn't lost the same sweet

twinkle in her eyes, nor the hearty chuckle that he fondly remembered. It felt good to be back with his family.

There's no place like home!

Mornings were a struggle in the O'Neill household. Coaxing little sleepyheads from their beds and somehow managing to have them dressed, fed, and out the door in time for school was not a job for the faint-hearted. Elsie dished up hot and hearty bowls of oatmeal laden with raisins and cinnamon for the family, still thinking about the "visit" from Jack in the wee hours of the morning. His brief yet pointed message, *"Be careful ..."* still made her shiver.

Setting a steaming bowl in front of Bobby, she remembered how much Jack had wanted a son. After his death, she was determined to make his dream come true. God bless Sister Faith and Charles for making it possible. The faint image of an Amish young lady came to mind—the one who had tearfully relinquished the gurgling blue bundle to Elsie's longing arms. *Does she cry herself to sleep? Is she thinking of him now?* She dreaded the day when the kids would start to question why they looked nothing alike—the day when Bobby might discover the truth of his roots. She'd made a promise to the girl, and to herself, which she fully intended to keep.

Bobby shoveled globs of oatmeal into his chubby cheeks, dripping half of it on his clean shirt, while Wilma dreamily stirred hers around in the bowl with a soup spoon. The hall clock chimed half-past the hour. "Speed it up, kids! We have to leave soon," Elsie's patience was running thin. "Bobby, look at you! Now we have to find a clean shirt! And Wilma, stop dawdling and eat your breakfast before it gets any colder."

Wilma snapped out of her woolgathering to ask, "Mommy, what does A-M-O-U-R spell?"

Startled, Elsie raised her eyebrows. "Why on earth would you ask that, honey?"

"She's been snooping in Auntie Marie's notebook!" Bobby spouted out the accusation along with a mouthful of mushy oats.

Marie gasped and locked eyes with her guilt-ridden niece.

Furious about being double-crossed, Wilma yelled at the spying little fink, "Mind your own beeswax, Bobby O'Neill! You promised not to tell!"

Her brother said she was "full of applesauce," and a shouting match ensued between the squabbling pair.

"Children, "Pipe down!" Their mother scolded. "Level with me, Wilma. Did you read Marie's journal?"

The little culprit hung her head, nodding to the affirmative, as tears began streaming down her flushed face. When Marie asked her why she'd invaded her privacy, Wilma wailed loudly and confessed that curiosity had gotten the best of her. "I didn't understand most of it, anyway. I'm sorry, Auntie Marie."

After reprimanding her daughter for being so nosey, Elsie turned to Marie and reminded her of another little girl who'd done the same thing a decade earlier.

"That's true," Marie sheepishly giggled at the memory. "It seems the shoe is on the other foot!"

Marie squatted next to Wilma, drying the little one's tears on a napkin, before giving her a smooch on the cheek. "I forgive you, sweetie. I used to read your Mommy's diary when she wasn't looking, too, so I'm the last one to pass judgment."

Wilma sniffled and looked up at her aunt with watery eyes, "Did you write about *that* in your notebook?"

"As a matter of fact, I did. Finish your breakfast, and I'll be right back."

After a few minutes of rummaging through a box under her bed, Marie found one of her earliest journals, blew off the dust, and carried it to the kitchen.

"I'll read you one of my entries, but then you have to scoot off to school." The O'Neill trio waited expectantly for Marie to begin. After flipping through a few pages, she recited in an expressive and animated tone:

> In trouble again, Dear Diary!
> But I just couldn't resist
> Snooping at my sister's private thoughts
> Of the blue-eyed beau she'd kissed.
> Mad as a hornet, she flew at me,
> So I darted outside through the hall;
> Climbed up the oak in the nick of time,
> To hear Elsie's shrieking call:
> "Come out, you brat, wherever you are!
> You'll be the death of me yet!
> I'll slap you silly, you nosey thing,
> And that's not an idle threat!"
> Waiting for Mama to rescue me,
> I perched on a leafy shelf.
> Hard as I try to be a good girl,
> I can't seem to help myself.

By the time Marie finished reading, everyone was laughing. Bobby stared at her in awe. "Did ya *really* used ta climb trees?" "And how! And I have the scars to prove it! As for you, Willie, I'm actually honored you wanted to read my journal ... but the next time, please ask first, okay?"

Wilma nodded while blowing her nose, and looked at Marie with glassy eyes. "I won't do it again. Promise! Will you teach me how to write like that, Auntie?"

"I'd love to, but first things first. Time for school!"

"Sister" to him in more than title, she'd providentially shown up at his most vulnerable time—abandoned and crying out for the love of a real family. She'd been his closest friend and confidante ever since. Watching her now, as she daintily swallowed a bite of Eggs Benedict, Charles thought back to their early years together. He remembered her flowing butterscotch hair, now cropped and humbly concealed beneath the snug-fitting wimple.

"In the old days, everyone assumed we'd end up together, because of our strong friendship."

The former Margaret Kathleen smiled affectionately at him. "Yes, but it wasn't God's plan, was it?"

"No, even at the age of twelve, I knew your heart was already spoken for, and that our love for each other was meant to be that of brother and sister."

Sister Faith fingered the plain gold band on her right hand, smiling wistfully. "Yes, it seems I knew what my calling was early on."

They spent a long time reminiscing about the past and some of the other kids they'd grown up with. One in particular came to mind—a girl from India who was close in age to Margaret Kathleen. Mirin was as lovely and joyful as the meaning of her name, "happiness."

Mirin's only possessions from her former life were kept in a steamer trunk at the foot of her bed, which contained several beautiful saris made with her departed mother's hands. As precious as they were to her, Mirin loved sharing them with the other girls for dress up. She taught them traditional dances from her homeland, and found pleasure in watching the other girls wearing the colorful pink, gold, turquoise and lavender saris as they told stories through stylized body and facial gestures.

"Whatever happened to Mirin?" Charles wondered. "It's been awhile since you mentioned her."

"I'm happy to report," Faith answered, "that Mirin is now a dance instructor and costume designer at the local performing arts studio where she met her husband. She's the mother of three beautiful children."

Charles was glad Mirin led a rich and full life. It was good to know her life had such a happy outcome—which was not the case for all children who passed through the doors of the Orphanage of the Holy Infant.

Charles rarely spoke to anyone but Sister Faith about his own early history. He was the only child of Raymond and Lorraine Hollister. His father worked long, hard shifts at the Rockford rail yards as a switch operator to put bread on his family's table, leaving his wife to carry the brunt of the household burdens. Lorraine had suffered from chronic depression after giving birth to Charles. Lonely nights without Ray drove her deeper into despondency and the forbidden bottle of hooch she kept hidden under the kitchen sink. Ray came home one morning to find his house a shambles, his wife out cold, and their five-year old digging through the garbage pail for his breakfast. He finally resigned himself to the inevitable, and wasted no time making arrangements to admit Lorraine to the New York State Inebriate Asylum. At his wits end about his son's welfare, he sought the help of an old friend, Sister Agnes of Holy Infant. Ray promised Charles he would visit often and that Lorraine would come for him when she was better. He did visit on special occasions, at least for the first several years—but "Mommy" never came.

When Charles was twelve years old, Ray broke the news of Lorraine's suicide and his plans to remarry. After that, his visits were few and far between ... eventually stopping altogether, with the exception of occasional letters. The only information Charles now had was an address in Lombard, and the name of his half-sister, Caroline. Prior to Charles's high school graduation, Raymond came into a sizeable inheritance, making it possible for him to fund his son's tuition at the University of Chicago. He'd shown up four years later when Charles received his degree in Business; but in spite of promises to stay in touch, Charles never saw him again. Knowing his father was a good man who loved him and did the best he could, Charles harbored no ill-will against him. Nevertheless, he'd chosen to let sleeping dogs lie and not intrude upon his father's life. As for his mother, he believed she didn't want him and had abandoned him—not once, but twice.

Then there was Patrice Willoughby, who'd left him high and dry at the altar while she traipsed off to Bermuda with some greasy gigolo. Her parents didn't think Charles was good enough for their daughter (born with a silver spoon in her mouth), but they would have preferred him over the smooth-tongued loser her fickle-as-a-weathervane heart fell for. *Live and learn!*

Charles would scoff when Sister Faith suggested that his past experiences of rejection might be at the root of his commitment issues; yet he knew she was right, as usual.

Sister Eymard refilled their coffee cups as Faith interrupted his reveries. "This visit is a long time coming, Chuck. You've only been back a couple of times since we arranged Bobby's adoption five years ago."

"Time flies, Sister! Did you ever hear from Bobby's birth mother again ... the young Amish woman?"

Shaking her head, Sister Faith sadly replied, "No. I'm sure she's determined to have no further contact with us. In her community, those unfortunate situations are best left buried. She was terrified of the ban."

"Understandable," Charles commented. "I hope she's at peace knowing she did something good for her baby. Elsie's a wonderful mother."

Faith patted her pocket. "By the way, we recently received a newsy letter from Elsie. Remind me to share some of it with you before you leave." She chuckled merrily, "It sounds like the little ones keep her and Marie on their toes!"

At the mention of Marie's name, Charles instantly turned sullen. That did not escape the perceptive nun's notice. She fixed her eyes on him with an insightful expression; he knew what was coming.

"Chuck, when was the last time you went to Mass or confession?"

"Well, it's like this, Sister. I'm a busy man and life gets in the way. It's not that I don't believe in God ... I do, but he and I don't communicate very well. There's things I'd like to ask him, but I don't know where to start."

"Start right where you are. That's where God always meets us."

"I've made so many blunders. Why would God even give me the time of day, as flawed as I am?"

"Because, Chuck, God created us. He knows our shortcomings and loves to use us in spite of our frailties. His strength and power are made perfect in our weakness. I know you've heard that before; it's from the twelfth chapter of Second Corinthians. He longs for us to trust in Him, and when we do, life is exciting!"

This conversation made Hollister sweat. "Yes, I've heard all of that, but it's not easy for me. I haven't had much of a prayer life lately and really should get around to it one of these days. However, I came here hoping *you* would have the answers I'm looking for."

"So you're not here just to catch up. There's more to it, isn't there? Something's troubling you, Chuck. Care to talk about it?"

He hesitated for one brief moment, then charged into the matter he so desperately needed to get off his chest. "I never could hide anything from you! You were the first and only person I thought to ask about this mess. You see, I've made an idiot of myself again over a woman. This time, someone much younger. What I perceived and hoped to be a romantic interest in me, turned out to be nothing more than youthful flirtation. All the time she had her cap set for someone else, and now they're engaged to be married. How do I forget her and move on with my life?"

Appearing confused, Sister Faith asked, "Chuck, you wouldn't by chance be referring to Marie Middleton, would you?"

He tilted his head in wonderment. "How do you do that? I know you have connections in high places, but are you a mind reader, too?"

"So, it *is* Marie, then! But why are you so sure she's engaged? When did this happen?"

"Right before Labor Day. I saw the whole thing with my own two eyes. Her old beau blew into town and swept Marie off her feet with a sparkler. I could see it dazzling in the sunlight several yards away!"

Sister bore an amused smile. "*Before* Labor Day! And you didn't actually talk to her about it, did you?"

"What would be the use?" he grumbled. "She made her choice!" Then, with irritation, "Wipe that silly grin off your face! Can't you see I'm in pain?!"

Faith irritated him further with an uncontrolled giggle while reaching into her tunic pocket. She told him there was something he needed to know, and passed him the envelope addressed to herself from her sister-in-law, Elsie O'Neill. He warily took it from her outstretched hand and asked, "Are you sure I should read this?"

"You *must* read it!"

Chapter Ten

October 1, 1924

Dear Sister Faith (and all at Holy Infant),

I thought of you this morning, missing the autumn colors that I used to take for granted in the Midwest. Though the change in seasons is barely noticeable here on the West Coast, we're enjoying cooler temperatures, and everyone is thinking about homemade soup and apple pie. The kids have figured out that Halloween is right around the corner. Our new friend, whom the kids affectionately call "Grandma Millie," has graciously offered to create costumes for them: an aviator uniform for Bobby, and Raggedy Ann for Wilma (perfect with her reddish hair, don't you think?).

Those two keep Marie and me hopping! They're forever getting into mischief, but too cute to be angry with for long. I may have a blind spot when they're naughty, but can't help being a pushover! They're so precious and keep Jack alive in my heart.

I can't wait to tell you my latest news, although, it may be received with mixed feelings. You know your brother was, and always will be, the love of my life; but I've met someone—a wonderful man who has drawn me out of my grief and back into the land of the living. His name is Avery Weston. We met one afternoon at the hotel. He's a Hollywood agent and urged me to be screen tested. While it was an exciting experience, it hasn't led to anything, yet. Avery assures me that with experience and exposure to the right people in the industry, my face could appear on screen in the not too distant future. Isn't that exciting?! I finally have a new goal and direction for my life. Thank God for Marie filling in for me when I'm away from the kids, working two jobs and being coached by Avery. It's all to provide a better life for my children, of course.

Avery is terribly handsome and treats me like a queen! Marie hasn't met him yet, so has no opinion one way or the other. She's happy I'm moving on with my life, though. On the other hand, Auntie Madge seems to know a rounder by a similar name, so has cautioned me, in no uncertain terms. The man she referred to certainly cannot be MY Avery! I realize Auntie has my best interests at heart and love her for it, but she can be a worry wart at times.

Marie and Bradley Smythe had a parting of ways right before Labor Day. He came to town and they agreed what they feel for each other is not the kind of love to base a marriage on. She mentioned something about Brad not making her "tingle," so I'm guessing maybe someone else does. He gave her a beautiful violin-shaped pin with an amethyst stud— (her birthstone) as a token of his affection. Isn't that sweet? It's so sparkly and she wears it while teaching her violin students.

There I go, jumping ahead! Marie has some free time now that the children are in school, so she placed an ad for violin instruction and already has three pupils, plus Wilma. Well, one dropped out, but that's another story.

There's something else about Marie which I can't quite put my finger on. Although she was relieved about her break-up with Bradley, she seems depressed. I'm guessing it has something to do with the cat and mouse game she and Charles Hollister have been playing for months. Every time I think love is in the air, a storm cloud blows in.

Mother tells us Charles is in the Chicago area, indefinitely, and I don't think Marie has heard a word from him. He also seemed glum the last time I saw him. Perhaps he'll pay you a visit and confide whatever is troubling him. Your loving words of wisdom seem to do him good.

God bless you as you continue to serve the children of Holy Infant with the depth of love that can only come from faith in Christ. Give my love to the other Sisters. You mean the world to me!

Affectionately, Elsie

Charles was stunned, realizing he may have destroyed his chances with Marie from impulsively jumping to conclusions. "What a chump I am!" He sheepishly handed the letter back to his dear friend, shaking his head in mortification.

Sister Faith gently replied, "Chuck, our Heavenly Father sees the beginning, the end, and everything in between. Not so with His children. We tend to take life at face value, without having all the facts. Seeing everything from His perspective would rule out faith and hope, wouldn't it? One day we'll see fully. For now, He gives us only a dimly-lit mirror. It's all a part of His plan for us to depend on Him as we learn and grow. Don't be too hard on yourself. Nothing breaks that God can't fix, and His mercies are new with each day that dawns."

Charles managed to crack a smile. "How *nunly* of you, to put it that way! I know you're right, but I can't help kicking myself. Back to Elsie, though. She's always been a little sheltered and naive, but the screen test business seems out of character for her. I may need to check out this Weston fellow myself, to be sure he's on the up-and-up."

Sister Faith nodded in agreement. "My thoughts, exactly. I'm worried about her, too."

"As for Marie," he continued, "if there's even a chance we're meant for each other, then all I want to do right now is *run* back to Coronado!"

Faith gleefully clasped her hands over her heart, "Do it! And go with God!"

A trail of hungry customers stretched out the door and onto the sidewalk; the mouth-watering aroma of roasting sausage and fish was hard to resist. Luckily, Marie and her date had arrived at Callahan's early enough to be near the front of the line. Their frazzled hostess, Mitzi, escorted them to a corner booth and handed them menus.

Marie smiled warmly at Elsie's counterpart. "You're awfully busy tonight!"

"Si, a normal Friday crowd and I'm missing Elsie *mucho*, but it's her turn for a night off. Who's looking after the niños?"

"They're with Mrs. Gable," Marie explained. "She's fitting them for their Halloween costumes. She's so good with them and they adore her so much that it almost makes me jealous sometimes! And yes, Elsie was glad to get the night off for her date with Avery."

Mitzi squinted at her and frowned. "Have you met this Señior Weston?"

"Not yet, Mitzi, but he seems to make Elsie happy, so he must be pretty special."

"Hmmm ... *special.* That's one way to put it!" Mitzi heard Paddy's not so subtle "Ha-hum!" Looking over her shoulder at her boss, she excused herself, assuring her guests their waitress would be with them *pronto.*

Once Maritza was out of earshot, Jonathan asked, "What's eating *her?*

"Oh, that's Mitzi for you. She loves to sleuth and is protective of my sister. She has a good heart and means well, but Elsie's a big girl who can take care of herself."

Jonathan patted his growling stomach. "I'm starving! Let's see what's on the menu. I could eat a horse!"

As they perused the selections, a perky brunette holding an order pad approached their booth. "Hi! I'm Caty, with a C! Are you ready to order?"

Jonathan's eyes shot up. "Caty with a C? Cathleen Callahan! Long time no see!"

Caty replied with equal delight, "Aye, Jonathan. Good to see ya! It *has* been a month o' Sundays!"

Jonathan explained that he'd recently returned from "up north," and then introduced Marie as his violin instructor. Caty and Marie acknowledged each other with customary hellos. Jonathan kept the conversation flowing, "It hadn't dawned on me you'd still be around here after all these years, but I haven't forgotten you or the rest of the gang at good old Coronado High."

Caty flushed. "Nor I, Jonathan. Those were bonnie times."

Marie made the connection and interjected. "You must be a sister to my newest violin student, Maggie Rose. She told me she has five siblings."

"Aye," Caty replied, "we're a big clan, we are. Maggie's got herself in a dither practicin' for her lesson tomorrow."

"Well, she's a darling girl, Caty, and a promising musician, too. She has a bright future. You must be so proud of her."

Her gray-blue eyes beamed as Caty exuberantly replied, "Aye! I'm poppin' me buttons!" Miss Callahan's flush deepened. She pulled the pencil from behind her ear and got down to business. "So what will it be tonight? Our specials are Bangers and Mash, and Roasted Salmon with Shamrock Salad. The soup of the day is Colcannon."

Marie appeared stumped. "Colcannon? I'm not familiar with that. What is it?"

"It's a yummy cream broth with potatoes, leeks and cabbage. My favorite," Caty explained.

"Bangers and Mash for me," Jonathan piped up. "I've been craving Mr. C's cooking for seven years! Authentic Irish grub as good as his is hard to come by. How about you, Marie?"

She ordered the salmon special, but declined the included choices of Irish brown, beer, or soda breads. Jonathan, on the other hand, asked for a serving of each.

"Comin' right up!" Caty managed a slightly shaky smile before taking the order slip to the kitchen.

Paddy, whom Marie had seen eyeing them all this time while sucking on the tip of his pipe, wasted no time in approaching their table. "Johnatin Woods! As I live and breathe! Where'd ya run off ta all these years, keepin' me poor girl pinin' away fer ya?!"

Jonathan looked embarrassed as he glanced back and forth between his date and Paddy. "Now, Mr. C., you *know* I've been away at school and didn't exactly run off!"

Caty who had undoubtedly overheard the conversation while returning with the drink tray, looked like she wished the floor would open and swallow her whole. "Oh Da! Don't be shamin' me, now!"

Once the Callahans had excused themselves, Marie studied Jonathan with great interest and a twinge of jealousy. "So, Caty was your high school sweetheart, wasn't she?"

Swallowing a swig of hot coffee, "Um, yeah. I guess you could say that. How astute of you! We dated, but agreed to go our separate ways after graduation to see where life would lead."

"Seems like life led you back to Coronado *and* to Caty."

"And to *you*, Marie. We *do* make beautiful music together, don't we?" He leaned over with a disarming smile and nudged her shoulder.

Marie playfully pushed him away. "You're such a corny charmer, but I like you best as a friend, for now. You see, I'm more or less on the rebound, and it wouldn't be fair to you or anyone else if I even considered a serious relationship for the time being. I'm not even sure if I *want* a relationship at this point. It could cramp my independence. In fact, it's highly probable that I'm meant to remain single. Can we take it slow?"

She'd clearly burst his bubble. "I knew something was holding you back," he said. "I hope you'll reconsider, but I won't rush you and am willing to wait. I want to be so much more to you than just a friend, Miss Middleton."

"Thank you, Jonathan. I do need time, but make sure someone isn't holding *you* back, either. We need to be 100 percent sure we're right for each other before moving forward. Perhaps you should reevaluate your feelings for Cathleen Callahan. She's obviously still smitten with you, and I really don't want to get hurt again."

Friday night, date night ... for everyone but Stanley Harrison, or so it seemed. He pulled his spectacles from his suit coat pocket to read the fine print on the movie poster for *Captain Blood*. Hearing a scuffle, his attention was diverted to a couple emerging from the theater's basement level door.

"No more hard to get, Goodie Two Shoes! It's time for me to make a *real* woman of you!"

"You've had too much to drink. Please take me home!" A strained, familiar female voice floated up to him.

The male voice gruffly replied, "I'll take you home, all right! To *my* home, Room 302 at The Del!"

Stanley watched as the thug in the shadows grabbed the protesting woman by the arm, nearly dragging her up the steps to the street-level walkway. "No! No!" she hysterically cried out.

Elsie ...?

The couple was now illuminated by the street lamp, and Stanley identified Elsie and the wolf in sheep's clothing he'd seen her with at the beach party. Adrenalin suddenly kicked in. He swiftly moved away from the window, taking a firm stance in front of Weston. Elsie nearly collapsed with relief.

"Hey, Buster! The lady said '*no*,' or don't you know the meaning of the word?"

Weston squinted through bleary-looking eyes and eventually recognized Harrison. "Oh! *You* again, Four Eyes! I see you don't have your ferocious doggy with you, so watcha gonna do about it?"

Stanley calmly removed his glasses, slid them into his breast pocket, and clenched his fists prepared to fight.

"What a joke! I bet you're blind as a bat without your widdow gwasses!" Weston started prancing around like a prize fighter in a mocking fashion. Staggering, Avery swung and missed; but Stanley swung back and connected with Weston's smarmy sneer. Sprawled flat as a pancake on the pavement, cradling his bloody jaw, Weston stammered, "L-lucky punch!"

Stanley patted his pocket with a wry smile, "They're only for reading."

"What's the trouble here?" At last, a police officer arrived on the scene.

"That maniac tried to kill me!" Weston whined. "It was totally unprovoked. My lady friend and I were minding our own business when he ambushed us and attacked me!"

"That's not true!" Elsie loudly contradicted. "Officer, the man on the ground tried to harm *me,* and this brave gentleman came to my rescue. Pointing an accusing finger at Weston, "He swung first, so it was clearly self-defense. His name is Avery Weston!"

"Weston, huh? We've been looking for you and your little band of hoodlums for weeks." The officer blew his whistle, signaling other cops at nearby locations to swarm in.

"They're running a speakeasy downstairs, too!" Elsie breathlessly informed them.

"I'll get you for this, pantywaist," Weston threatened Stanley. "And you, too, stool pigeon!" He shot a menacing glare at Elsie, who now cowered behind Harrison. "You don't know who you're dealing with! No one finks on me and gets away with it!"

"*We* know who you are—got the goods on you, louse!" the officer informed him. "With your record, you won't be making good on those threats any time soon. Cuff him!" Two of the officers restrained Weston and led him to a patrol car, as the others headed to the basement—pistols drawn.

While the police did their job, a tearful, shaking Elsie turned to Stanley. "You saved my life! He was planning to force himself on me, or worse. How can I ever thank you?"

Harrison's calm expression belied the rapid heart palpitations. "Well ..." he slowly drawled. "I *was* planning to see this movie. Care to join me?"

Saturday morning's bold headline caused Marie's jaw to drop in horror. "Elsie, look at this! Are they talking about *you*?"

With a groan, Elsie peeked over her sister's shoulder. This was not the kind of publicity she'd counted on getting through Avery Weston. Not the scandal sheet!

LOCAL HERO KNOCKS-OUT CRIME!

Coronado citizen, Stanley Harrison, saved a young mother's life and inadvertently exposed a downtown speakeasy on the night of October 10, 1924. Harrison, (a local accountant), single-handedly took down a long sought-after criminal, who currently goes by the name of Avery Weston (A.K.A. Wes Avery, Ray West, among other aliases) and is known to prey on unsuspecting women seeking Hollywood films careers. To protect her privacy, Weston's victim shall remain nameless. Mild-mannered Harrison, who will be honored by our esteemed Chief of Police, Eugene Martin, at the next meeting of the City Hall, was quoted as saying, "Well, I came downtown to see Captain Blood, and looks like I found him!" Harrison is, without a doubt, one of Coronado's finest. Per arresting Officer Ben Daniels, wily Weston will be incarcerated at an undisclosed detention facility upon arraignment.

(By Jeff Dylan, Cub Reporter, *and Coronado Eagle & Journal*)

"At least they didn't print my name." Elsie uttered in relief. "It would have been beyond humiliating. I can't believe I was so naive and gullible! I totally chose to ignore all the warning signs, and I won't blame Auntie Madge and Mitzie if they say, 'I told you so.'"

"This is terrifying! Did that brute hurt you, sister?"

Elsie dropped the shoulder of her silky lounging robe, revealing her badly bruised upper arm. "He tried to, but Stanley appeared from nowhere and came to my rescue. You should have seen him; he was cool as a cucumber! Stanley looked the scoundrel straight in the eye and socked him in the jaw! I could be dead right now, or wishing I were! Avery threatened retaliation, too, Marie! I'm scared to death and can only pray they lock him up for the rest of his life!"

Wilma and Bobby had thrived in the California sunshine and fresh air, and were growing by leaps and bounds—along with their appetites. Keeping the pantry stocked had become quite a challenge. "Cereal, sugar, ground beef, lettuce ..." Marie made a final review of her shopping list before checking out. Luckily, items like milk, eggs, bread and ice were delivered directly to their front porch. The grocery bag bulged at the seams, but home was only a few blocks away. Exiting Petersons' mom-and-pop market, the screen door swung behind her with its bell jangling. With a jarring thud, she'd crashed into a brick wall! At least it felt like one. Peeking beneath her bulging grocery sack to hunt for an item which had sprung out, she spied a pair of shiny brown Florsheims. "Hey, Mister! Watch where you're going!" "I beg your pardon?" a perturbed-sounding male voice objected (a voice she'd know anywhere).

Be still, my heart! Lowering her over-loaded bag, their eyes met: sky blue and coal black.

"Good morning, Cary," she greeted him, as nonchalantly as possible.

"Good day to you, too, Miss Middleton! Fancy running into *you* here!" He gallantly tipped his hat with a mischievous grin.

By now, she'd lowered the bag enough to see more of his face than from the nose up, and burst into a fit of hysterics. "What on Earth have you done to yourself?!"

His hand stroked his scruffy chin. "Madam, could you possibly be referring to my beard?"

Wincing from a stitch in her side, "Well, perhaps the *beginning* of one! You look like a derelict!" she tittered.

He glowered! "A *derelict?!* What a lousy thing to say! Will you never grow up?" He stuffed the stray box of baking soda back into her parcel, spun on his heels, and stormed off, grumbling, "Should've stayed in Chicago!"

Chapter Eleven

Life seemed to be filled with "if onlies" for the Middleton girls. If only Jack could come home, if only Elsie hadn't fallen for Weston's deception, if only Mama and Pops weren't so far away, and if only Marie had kept her big mouth shut and not made fun of Cary's sprouting beard!

She'd expected him to be gone much longer, so how could Marie have possibly prepared herself for the way they literally bumped into each other? After all, he *did* look ridiculous with the coarse, black stubble erupting from his chin: the once beautiful, smooth, firm chin with an adorable crater dead center. His dimple meant everything to her! It was the spot she would focus on to prevent contact with those soulful eyes which made her swoon. It was the contour she longed to trace with her finger tips, but didn't have the nerve. Now it would be hidden under a carpet of sharp and shaggy bristles, making him more untouchable than ever. The thought of caressing—or Heaven forbid, kissing—such a scratchy face was not at all appealing, even it if was *Cary's* face! But it *was* Cary's face, and he had a right to do with it as he pleased, she supposed. Like it or not, she had no real claim on him.

She'd been crushed when Cary left town with only a grim nod, right before the trolley swept him away. A door had been rudely slammed in her face! Not knowing where he was for a full week had been agonizing, until Mama inadvertently revealed his whereabouts in her letter. Marie hoped and prayed for a chance to clear the air between them. When more time passed by with no word, she'd decided to chase away her blues with the fun-loving Jonathan Woods. Then, coming face to face with Cary, at last, the feelings she'd tried so hard to bury had been revived, and she'd messed things up, again. He seemed to bring out the scamp in her (the exasperating child within). *Will you never grow up?!* The echo of his scorn made her cringe.

Marie couldn't deny that Jonathan was definitely in the mix, tugging at her emotions and heart strings. Maybe Suz was right, and stuffy old Cary needed someone closer to his own age and experience; whereas she needed a younger man like funny and flirtatious Jonathan, who boldly made his attraction for her clear, and laughed with abandon. But she wasn't *exactly* in love with Jonathan. She vowed her next meeting with Cary—if there was one—would be different. She would behave herself; and if he tried to stomp off again, she'd be right behind him. They'd have it out once and for all! *If only I'd been born a decade sooner.* Aloud, she softly whimpered into the autumn breeze, "I miss you, my dusky shadow."

It took a lot of elbow grease, but scrubbing the scum from the bathtub of the infamous room number 302 was far easier than washing away the memory of Friday night. Elsie felt dirty just thinking about it. Her skin crawled by being in Avery's vacated room: not only from cleaning up the filth he'd left behind, but from rumors of this room being haunted by the ghost of a former hotel guest, Kate Morgan, who allegedly shot herself on the hotel's exterior steps leading to the beach in 1892. But then again, was it suicide after all, or did poor Kate have her own Avery Weston?

Scrubbing the porcelain in a frenzy, Elsie kept glancing over her shoulder. She had the heebie-jeebies ... like she was being watched! She tried to calm her nerves. *Just my overactive imagination.* Even so, she was grateful for the rays of sunlight streaming through the windows. This was the very room in which she might have been raped. She'd been too *cabezon* (stubborn), as Mitzie would say, to heed the warnings of those who cared about her, including Jack. She'd even dismissed the red flags Weston himself had waved before her blinded eyes. What started out as a fun and glamorous Friday evening quickly turned ugly and terrifying. Being ushered into a secret, underground world had made her prickle with excitement. She was living on the edge and felt deliriously daring and alive.

The Casanova had trotted her around, displaying his latest conquest. Between a tango and a foxtrot, he'd obtained drinks through a peculiar sliding drawer in the wall (men on both sides "speaking easy" to avoid identification). Weston laughed at her for refusing the foul-smelling beer, and downed both glasses himself. His next trip to the bar was for something stronger (a MacGyver, he'd said), which she also declined. Each shot made him less and less enthralled with his teetotaler date; his speech turned abusive. When she'd begged to leave, Avery relented, with a sinister plan in mind. His leering, repulsive grin as he dragged her up the staircase made her sick to her stomach.

Thank God for placing Stanley outside the theater at that precise moment, or she dreaded to think what would have happened

next. He was like a guardian angel the way he staunchly confronted her plastered escort. Stanley never flinched when Avery swung, but took down his ruthless adversary with one swift, well-directed punch. The calm manner in which Stanley had asked her for a date in the midst of total chaos was so matter of fact it seemed perfectly normal—further demonstrating his confident inner strength. Elsie had no idea her mild-mannered cafe patron had so much going for him ... definitely more than met the eye. Unlike Avery, Stanley made her feel safe and comfortable. Was that enough? *Oh Jack ... if only!*

Charles Hollister scrutinized his face in the bathroom mirror, while events of the past few days and the annoying run-in with Marie ran through his head.

After his enlightening conversation with Sister Faith, Charles hopped onto the first train to the West Coast, impatiently counting off each of the 2,000 miles which separated him from his destiny. How he'd envied men like Orville Wright and Charles Lindbergh who could take to the air at will in their flying machines. Driving would not have shortened the trip, but would have been more pleasant than sharing a cramped and stuffy rail car with total strangers.

"Old Girl" had been faithful and served him well for over a decade, so he'd dragged his feet about trading in his aging flivver for a later model. He'd admired his colleagues who cruised through town in their snazzy new McFarlans, Stutz Bearcats, and other eye-catching touring cars. Money wasn't the issue; he hadn't been able to commit to a particular make and model. *Story of my life!* It was high time to shop around for a new machine.

He'd raced to the hotel to freshen up before knocking on the red cottage door. No answer. *She must be dropping the kids off at school.* Strolling through town, looking from left to right, he'd crashed smack dab into the object of his search. How quickly pleasure had turned to irritation. Pride had gotten the best of him, so he'd stalked off, not even offering to carry the chock-full grocery sack he'd nearly knocked from her arms.

Charles pulled a ruler from the cupboard next to the sink and measured the latest growth: a quarter of an inch in two days! Pleased with the progress, he peered closer at his reflection. *What's that?!* He yanked on it and winced. Sure enough, a gray hair! As much as he hated to admit it, Marie was right. He *did* look like a derelict!

He moistened his shaving brush and swished it in the mug of bar soap before lathering up his jaws. If only he could slice Marie from his being so easily. She was imbedded deeper under his skin than those confounded whiskers.

"Trick or Treat!!" Marie accompanied Elsie and her little beggars while making their neighborhood rounds.

Halloween had arrived without further contact with Cary. She'd made a few attempts to connect, but kept missing him. The one time she did spot him from a distance, he was with Jayne Blackwell. Marie chose not to confront them, unable to bear the humiliation of another spurning. For now, all she could do was ask Elsie to deliver another note to Cary at The Del, and wait for a response or an opportunity to clear the air with Cary in private.

As for Jonathan, he'd kissed her last week, and she'd kissed him back. It was a very nice kiss—better than Bradley's—but something was missing ... the tingle. She'd closed her eyes and waited for it, but it didn't happen. Marie knew in her heart it wasn't fair to keep Jonathan dangling much longer. She had to make a decision.

Marie drew her attention back to Wilma and Bobby who now proudly sported the costumes Grandma Millie had designed for them. Bobby, wearing his aviator suit, soared down the block, arms outspread and loudly roaring like a plane engine; Wilma's red locks bounced while emulating the flopping movements of a rag doll.

Emotion welled in Elsie's eyes as she witnessed her children's joyful antics. "Aren't they cute, Marie? So cute it hurts!"

"The cutest kids in Coronado, Elsie! But they come from two good sets of genes."

Elsie gazed at the horizon as the last rays of sunlight dipped behind it. "Marie, do you think the people in Heaven can see us? Do you suppose *Jack* can see them now?"

"I'm not sure, Elsie, but it's a comforting thought. Whether he can or not, you're doing a wonderful job on your own. He'd be very proud of you."

"Thanks, Marie, but it's really hard being a mother *and* a father. They need a daddy. I owe it to them."

At that moment, Arnold Wilcox approached, wearing a gaudy acrobat getup and chomping on a mouthful of gooey sweets. His over-bearing mother trailed behind her little holy terror with a flashlight trained on him. "No more candy, Arnie! You'll rot your teeth!" Her incorrigible son dismissed her concern, by yelling back "Malarkey!" At the sight of his ex-violin instructor, he exposed a chocolaty grin. "Get a load of this, Doll!" He then vaulted a picket fence with the ease of an alley cat.

The slightly winded Mrs. Wilcox shot an icy glare at Marie in passing, before shrilly addressing her agile boy. "Arnieee! You mustn't overexert yourself! And please try not to injure your delicate hands. I haven't insured them yet!"

"So that's the famous Arnold Wilcox?!" Elsie observed the pair in drop-jawed astonishment. "As Mother would say, *that's rare!*"

Auntie Madge had returned to Hollywood, promising to stay in touch with her nieces. She was immensely relieved to know the little affair between Elsie and Weston had ended, with Weston being where he couldn't hurt a fly—at least for the foreseeable future. Madge Middleton came across as a tough cookie with her glitzy, high-brow exterior, but possessed a most tender heart and soul. Elsie had tearfully apologized to Madge for losing her temper and disregarding her aunt's intuition. They'd parted with an affectionate hug; all was forgiven.

It seemed most of Coronado's predominantly Republican population was at the beach this glorious weekend, in celebration of President-Elect Calvin Coolidge's landslide victory. Basking in the warmth of the radiant sunshine, who would have believed this was early November? Marie admired her tanned, bare legs stretched out from her bathing costume, fully aware of the nearby handsome life guard who was ogling her. Oh, what would Mama say? But Mama wasn't here, neither was Pops, and thankfully not Elsie, since Marie was wearing *her* bathing costume. She knew she'd catch it from her older sister for borrowing the suit without even asking. Too bad Elsie had to work on Saturdays, or she'd be initiating the brand new costume herself. *C'est la vie!*

(That's life!) What was the harm? Sitting serenely on the blanket wouldn't hurt it one bit.

Wilma and Bobby scooped sand with toy shovels near the water's edge, forming a deep trough for remnants of the incoming waves to trickle through. Their delighted squeals made her heart swell with tender emotion. Marie remembered the morning when Willie had confessed to reading her journal and asked what A-M-O-U-R meant. Love. . . . "How do I spell love?" Marie whispered. She wrote in the sand with her index finger, then underlined the letters L-O-V-E. Underneath, she inscribed Wilma, Bobby, Elsie ... then paused as a wave of longing for Mama and Pops engulfed her. Perhaps another "Dear All" letter would be in their mailbox this afternoon. Gazing beyond the children, past the breakers, she spotted a familiar vessel. "That's how I spell love." She dug her finger back into the sand and carved his name. Jonathan Wood's name hadn't made the list, because today's thoughts were of the elusive Charles Hollister. Her jumble of emotions flip-flopped between love and annoyance. Somehow, merely *liking* him was impossible. *I guess I love you too much to start liking you,* she whispered with her eyes riveted on the blue and white sailboat being propelled across her line of vision by the balmy breeze. *Such a pretty picture!* Feeling inspired, she opened her journal and completed a poem she'd begun earlier with words so private she'd written them in French:

À mon bon ami, Charles Hollister

> Si je ne tu avais jamais rencontré,
> Et nous étions separe des océans,
> Il y aurait encore être ce désir douloureux
> Pour tu de tenir, dans mon cœur.

Mais je me r'appelle de toi pour toujours;

Et si tu n'est pas loin,

Vagues de engloutissement de la peur se noient

J'ai du mal à dire:

Tu est beau, mon cher!

Tu est le personne le plus importante pour moi.

Mon amour pour toi est insondable—

Plus profond que n'importe quelle mer.

Je suis en amour avec toi, Cary.

Dites moi, s'il te plais que tu m'aimes.

It couldn't be twelve o'clock already!? The Angelus bells faintly tolled from distant Sacred Heart Church, announcing the noon hour. As Marie jumped to her feet, the journal slipped off her lap onto the sand. Squinting against the sun's glare on the water, the only trace of the kids was little footprints leading into the foamy surf. Her heart was clutched by fear.

Marie glanced over her shoulder, and prayed her sister wasn't coming her way. Not yet! Elsie was due at any moment, and Marie knew The Del's head housekeeper was a stickler for punctuality. Elsie's break would be on time, and she'd come directly to the waterfront to play with her children at the beach—where a few seconds ago, Wilma and Bobby had been at her side. She'd taken her eyes off them for only a second ... a minute or two at the most! Where were they? She feared the worst, for they truly had vanished! Marie raced toward the water, her heart in her throat, eyes darting through the crowd of revelers. She looked back toward the tower, but now the lifeguard was missing, too! *For crying out loud!* She spotted him yards away, flexing his muscles for a gaggle of silly-goose bathing beauties, with his back to the water.

In sheer terror, her eyes darted over the waves until a big white hair bow caught her eye. There! "Wil-ma!" Marie's voice, tight with fear and anger, startled the swimmers around her. She called more loudly, "Wil-ma!!" The bobbing head with the drenched white bow turned toward her. Terrified hazel peepers met Marie's anguished blue ones. "Auntie Marie!! Help!!"

Bringing his Skerry Cruiser about, Charles Hollister braced himself against the side of the sailboat. Cutting across the wind was a sure way to capsize his fifteen-by-five-foot boat, but there was no time to lose. He steered straight for the O'Neill kiddies who appeared to be in over their heads and gasping for air. And there was horrified Marie, trying to drag them from the clutches of the sea. What had started as a leisurely sail in the calmer waters beyond the pier, was now a test of every skill he possessed.

Curses, screams, and diving bodies made way for the sailboat flying toward shore with a madman at the helm. As he reached the first curling wave, the inevitable happened. His pretty blue and white sailboat capsized, sending Hollister flailing through the air like a duck with a broken wing. Fighting his way to the surface and clinging to his overturned vessel, a dozen screeching sea gulls mocked him overhead.

Marie reached her niece a moment later, snatched her from the water, and crushed the trembling little girl against her heaving chest. "Thank You, Jesus," she sobbed. But where was Bobby? At last, she spotted him and nearly collapsed with relief. Bobby had miraculously been swept to shore and seemed to be unharmed. Standing ankle-deep in wet sand, he looked at his aunt and grinned. "Mr. Hollister's boat almost runned me over! Did ya see it?" Marie's stomach dropped: both at the thought of the danger in which her inattention had placed the children, and of Cary hitting the cold salt water in an expensive, sporty outfit. This would not improve their relationship one iota. Even so, the sight of him *was* extremely entertaining!

Charles frantically scanned the shoreline for Marie and the kids. He was relieved, then furious, to see all three of them standing safe and sound on shore, squealing with laughter and pointing at their funny friend. Looking around, Hollister was mortified to discover he'd given the entire beach crowd a show they'd long remember. *He* certainly wouldn't forget it any time soon!

Elsie arrived in time to witness the tail end of the near catastrophe, and protectively herded her babies away from the water. Pausing at the umbrella under which Marie had been lounging minutes before, she snatched up her children's bundle of clothing and stormed off the beach, with her little ducklings waddling behind her. Suddenly, Elsie turned toward her sister, eyeball to eyeball, and snapped, "Don't think even for one *minute* I haven't noticed what you're wearing!"

Marie struggled to compose herself as she gathered up her belongings and stumbled behind her fuming sister. Footprints had obliterated the names in the sand, but love remained.

An hour later, after smoothing things over with Elsie, Marie realized her journal had been left behind. She raced back to the beach and was relieved to see it lying where she'd left it, flapping in the breeze. But when she picked it up, she was horrified to find the page she'd last written on had been ripped out. With a sinking heart she groaned, *What if . . .*

Cathleen Callahan was in a dither of emotions, being tormented by her own "if onlies." Seeing Jonathan again had stirred up feelings she'd tried so hard to suppress for the past several years. Her heart leapt in her throat the moment he entered her family's diner; but he hadn't even noticed her, being under the spell of the pretty blonde girl at his side.

It all began in their Sophomore English Class at Coronado High School. Seated across the aisle from each other, it didn't take long for Caty to become smitten with him. Aye, 'twas no denyin' his fiercely beguilin' features; but the attraction she felt for him was more than skin deep. Jonathan was upbeat, kind, and funny. His cute sense of humor made her giggle too much for their teacher's liking. They'd bury their noses in composition notebooks as spinsterish Miss Ralston peered in their direction through her pince-nez. "Class, *we* are having entirely too much fun! Silence, please!" Quite a pair, they were!

Her American-born classmates sometimes made Caty feel inferior or even stupid because of her thick Irish accent, but not Jonathan. He thought the way she spoke was charming, and he gallantly escorted her to every school function there was—treating her like a princess—which made the other girls turn Kelly green. He was that proud of her, he was!

On her sweet-sixteenth birthday, "Da" finally agreed to let them date ... first within the safety of the crowd they hung around with, and alone during their senior year. By then, Jonathan had wormed his charm into Ma'am and Da's hearts, too.

A bewilderin' day it was when Jonathan broke the devastating news to her. In the fall, he'd be going to college in Northern California with the goal in mind of earning a BA in Education and a teaching certificate. It could take several years. Her heart sank! There was no way she could join him—Da didn't make nearly enough for her to attend college. Like for most girls in her station of life, it had been assumed she'd marry and raise a family, with no need for higher education.

When Jonathan came home for the first Christmas break, he seemed detached from her. Weeks later, a rather formal letter came, stating that if she felt inclined to date someone else, he wouldn't hold it against her. She'd often wondered during the past several years how often *he'd* felt so inclined. As for her, she hadn't so much as taken a second gander at another laddie.

Himself had shown up out of the clear blue with someone else, dredging up the pain she'd felt when reading the letter so long ago. It stung when he'd addressed her like an old playmate, rather than his first love.

Caty heard rumors that Jonathan planned to stick around town while he hunted for a teaching position in the San Diego area. Not only had he earned his BA and teaching certificate, but a Masters, too. He'd done well for himself, and was no doubt looking for a highly-educated, sophisticated woman to share his life with ... not a fair-to-middlin' girl who held the same job since high school, working for her parents! *It's ashamed, I should be!* She wondered what the accomplished Miss Middleton thought of her, or if she knew that Jonathan had been *her* dearie.

If only I'd begged him not to leave seven years ago! If only Da had seen fit to send me off to college with Jonathan. Should she have followed Jonathan anyway, no matter what? At the time, she could do no such shameless thing. Hard as it was when he was far away, it was ever so much harder now. *How am I to bear it, seein' him 'round all the time, with me heart achin' and lovin' him so?* If only he would see fit to give her another whirl.

One person on the island was totally at peace this lovely autumn day—free of doubts and filled with hope. Stanley Harrison still marveled that he'd mustered the gumption to put Avery Weston in his place—spread out on the pavement, awaiting arrest. It had been surreal. In his wildest dreams, he wouldn't have imagined that evening to end with the beautiful Elsie O'Neill seated beside him in the dark theatre, clutching his arm for dear life while watching *Captain Blood*. Wonder of wonders, she'd even agreed to see him again! There was no guarantee of how their relationship would turn out; but now, he at least had a shot at winning her heart. No matter what the outcome, he would continue to place his trust in his faithful and loving Heavenly Father. *Thy will be done.*

Chapter Twelve

I'm here for only one reason, Charles reminded himself as he knocked on the red door. *Just checking on their welfare.* It had been no easy undertaking to right his capsized vessel, thinking at first it was a total loss. However, with the assistance of a few muscle-bound lifeguards, the Solitaire was recovering from her ordeal in dry dock.

After the Middleton group had left the beach, he'd noticed what looked like a book lying on the sand, in the very spot they'd hurriedly vacated. *Must have left something behind.* Bending over in his soggy nautical wear, he discovered it to be a journal filled with handwritten poetry. He picked it up, and on closer inspection it resembled Marie's pretty handwriting. To his surprise, the first page bore his own name. He couldn't decipher the rest of it, penned in a foreign language. *Looks like French. Has to be Marie's.* Impulsively, he'd torn the page from its binding, thinking she'd deserved it for poking fun at him again. Instantly, he'd regretted his rash action, knowing it would now be too embarrassing to return the journal. So he'd laid the book where he'd found it, crossing his fingers it would soon be back in her hands. Charles had deliberately chosen to ignore a growing pile of notes that Marie sent to him like clockwork on a daily basis. Today's incident had worn him down, and he'd talked himself into calling on little Mimi.

The wooden door creaked open, and there she stood—the one who'd been turning his life upside down since she was ten years old. Her skin was aglow from a warm soak in the tub, and her freshly-shampooed hair was wrapped in a terry cloth towel. She smelled great, too (like Lux Soap). *Could she possibly be more enchanting?*

Marie was obviously caught off guard, and tightened the belt of her chenille bathrobe. "Cary!?"

"Sorry to drop by unannounced, but I needed to make sure everyone is okay and apologize for making the situation in the water even worse."

"Not at all! We owe you for trying to save the children's lives." Then she winced. "As for your boat, is it gone?"

"Thanks to some alert life guards, she's no worse for wear. Should dry out well in this warm, sunny weather we're having." Marie said she found that bit of information amusing, since the only guard she'd seen had been too busy flexing his muscles to notice that Wilma and Bobby were in over their heads. She expressed relief that the vessel had been fished from the sea. "I was afraid your boat had been sacrificed for our welfare." Her gratitude and concern bolstered his courage. "What's most important is *your* safety."

An awkward silence passed between them before Marie glanced down at her apparel and blurted out, "I'd invite you in, but as you can see ... Elsie isn't home and the children are napping."

"No problem. Like I said, just checking on all of you." He stood there silently looking at her, making no move to leave, searching her eyes with his own. Had he been able to read her mind, he would have known this was the moment she'd prayed for. Marie excused herself to dress and prepare refreshments while Charles waited on the porch.

He moved across squeaking floor boards and helped himself to a roomy wicker chair. Sinking into it, he was relieved to spot the journal lying safely on a small patio table next to a letter addressed to Marie in Anna Middleton's handwriting. The missing journal page was now folded and tucked inside his billfold for safekeeping, until he could find a translator.

While waiting for his charming hostess to return, he took deep breaths of invigorating Glorietta Bay air and admired the cheerful pots of brightly-colored Martha Washingtons hanging from the eaves of the front porch. The girls had made this place home, with odds and ends they'd picked up (mostly second-hand, due to their limited resources).

Marie returned carrying a tray of coffee and homemade chocolate chip cookies, and carefully set it down on the large rattan ottoman.

Smiling at his now clean-shaven face, she expressed her remorse, "Sorry about calling you a derelict, and for laughing at you on the beach. I couldn't seem to help myself."

Charles chuckled, "When have you *ever* been able to help yourself, Mimi?!"

Marie's face grew warm as she continued. "The whole thing was my fault, entirely."

Charles paused before biting into a cookie and grinned, "That I can believe!" Marie playfully snapped him with a tea towel, and they shared a rare belly laugh together.

Lightly blowing on his steaming cup of joe, Charles made a proposition. Today's near disaster had reminded him of his promise to take the kids sailing. He suggested they could use some water safety instruction and swimming lessons. "I'm game for it if Elsie approves!" Marie promised to broach the subject that night, right after Elsie's shift at Callahan's.

Studying her face carefully, he added, "Of course, I'm afraid it will have to wait until sometime after the New Year, since I've been called to Paris on business for several weeks. I'm leaving right after Thanksgiving. It's not the best timing, but can't be helped." There it was ... exactly the expression he'd counted on ... disappointment.

Charles explained that Hugh had placed him in charge of a project to provide new suits of clothing for the many veterans who endured the effects of life-changing injuries. For them, the war continued to rage on. He'd soon be on his way to France for updates on men's fashion trends by attending expositions featuring haute couture designers such as Cristóbal Balenciaga and Salvatore Ferragamo. "Only the best for those who laid their lives on the line, and we're going to get it for them, no matter how long it takes."

Tears threatened to fall from Marie's glistening, blue eyes. "You're a good man, Cary ... better than I've given you credit for."

Her undeserved praise embarrassed him and triggered a hoarse reply, "Not at all." He felt a twinge of guilt for stealing her journal page. Charles took another swig of coffee and reached for his third cookie. "Zowie! These are fabulous! Are they from the bakery?"

Marie colored, "No, believe it or not, I baked them myself!" When his eyes widened in surprise, she admitted to not being able to take credit for them, since it was Nanette LaNell's signature cookie (whom after some arm twisting, had shared the recipe with Mama). It was now their own family's well-guarded *secret* recipe.

"Nanette's a real peach and a woman of many talents," Cary praised Hugh Middleton's best seamstress, and subconsciously glanced over at the journal. "I suspect you possess some hidden talents yourself, Miss Middleton!"

Marie's alarmed expression suggested he may have given himself away. He thought of some other writing she'd done recently, and knew an apology was in order.

"About your letters ... the ones piled up in my hotel room that I didn't even open. That was rude of me, and I apologize for it. Maybe one day I'll be able to explain it all to you."

It was definitely the break-through Marie had prayed for. "I did wonder why you didn't respond, but what matters now, Cary, is that you're here and we're friends again. We *are* friends, aren't we?"

Charles looked deeply into her pretty eyes with a deadpan expression. "Of course we are, Mimi. In fact, we have a very *sweet* friendship ... based on ice cream cones and chocolate chip cookies!" A grin broke across his face and he threw his head back in unbridled laughter!

"You rascal!" Marie loved seeing this rare side of him. "In that case, we're having some *friends* in for Thanksgiving dinner. It won't be like Mama's cooking, but we'll do our best. You'd be more than welcome to join us."

Marie's hopeful look made his heart melt like the gooey chips in the cookies. He said he just might take her up on it, because he hadn't eaten a home-cooked meal since his trip to Oak Park. When she suggested he bring along Jayne Blackwell, he replied with a knowing look, "*I'll* be there!"

⚜

Marie tingled with elation after her visit with Cary. She picked up her journal to finish the poem she'd begun on Labor Day, but spotted Mama's yet-unread letter. She set the notebook aside and tore open the envelope.

Chérie,

As you can see, this is not my usual group letter, but is meant for your eyes, only.

Your last cheerful message described humorous adventures that we laughed about for several days! You have a gift for writing.

One day (God willing) you will discover how gifted *mothers* are at reading between the lines. The blank spaces in your letters tell me what your heart most longs for: the love of one very special man. If that someone is whom I suspect he may be, you have chosen well, my daughter. May he prove to be your soul mate, as Hugh is mine.

Do not despair, Marie Jeannette. *Les affairs des coeur* (affairs of the heart) should not be rushed, but must be allowed to blossom in God's own time. You are so very young, and I pray there are many wonderful surprises in store for you. Always remember that the best surprises come through faith, believing all things are possible.

Distance cannot prevent me from hearing the cries of your longing heart. Listen to hope's persistent whisper and never give up on love, or your dream of a music career. I believe you can have the best of both worlds.

Wouldn't it be *merveilleux* to have a magic window, transcending time and space, through which we could enjoy little visits? Impossible, of course! Though we cannot change yesterday, or perhaps even today, we can always dream of tomorrow. *I* dream of my Dear All every night, and you are foremost in my prayers.

Je t'aime! (I love you)

Mama

At the bottom of the page, Anna had sketched a young couple—light hair and dark—holding hands in an open doorway. Marie marveled at her mother's insight. She touched the letter to her face and breathed in the comforting scent of Anna Middleton's signature French perfume. "I love you, Mama."

Feeling more confident than ever, she turned back to the Labor Day poem where she'd ended with, "My ears search for an echo of sound from that higher plane where *you* are," and continued:

> I listen until it comes at last . . .
> the faintest whisper on a breeze,
> drifting softly closer to my ear,
> speaking in feelings more than words.
> Peace caresses my aching brow,
> pristine waters quench my thirsty soul,
> giants are slain as you wave your hand.
> I can rest, knowing you are near.
> One day I'll hear you call my name;
> not a whisper, but a thund'ring shout!
> Hand and hand together we will fly.
> Until that time, I shall be content
> to waken with each dew-kissed dawn
> and bravely meet the task at hand.
> While angels paint the evening hues,
> anxiety is brushed away.
> Tomorrow is my friend—I am renewed.

She had another visit from Jack. This time, Elsie watched as he stamped the Toby Furniture trademark on the bottom of the beautiful French Moderne lamp table to be placed in Chicago's Palmer House (the hotel where they'd spent their wedding night). She remembered the single red rose he'd presented to her then, and on many other occasions, in token of his love. Jack was a highly skilled craftsman who took great pride in the pieces he produced. He was in the habit of whistling, and tonight it was *Molly Malone*. She loved the way his thick, straight, gingery hair swept across his forehead from the left side part. Looking up from his work, he grinned and winked a sparkling blue eye at his beautiful bride. As quickly as he'd appeared, he was gone—leaving behind the fading whistle, the distinct aromatic scent of saw dust, and overwhelming loneliness.

Their little charges were all tucked in and sleeping soundly. Last to go down was the newest foundling at Orphanage of the Holy Infant. Nellie Magnusson sobbed for the longest time, distraught over the loss of familiar faces and surroundings. Sister Faith softly stroked her arm and sang *Jesus Gentlest Saviour* until Nellie finally drifted off from sheer exhaustion. Her heart ached for the little girl, having felt the same sadness and confusion when she and Jack first came to Holy Infant. She was ten years old and her little brother five when their father's car was hit head-on. Miraculously, Margaret Kathleen and Robert "Jack" survived with only minor injuries, but both of their parents were killed instantly. With no family members able or willing to take them in, a social worker placed them in the care of Sister Agnes. In the long-run, it was the best possible thing to happen, in spite of the horrendous tragedy that would be forever imprinted on their memories.

While the household slumbered, the Sisters retired to their private sitting room to review the day's events and read the mail. Two wonderful letters had arrived that morning. Sister Faith slit open the envelope from Chuck first, anxious for news of his re-union with Marie. As she read his humorous narrative, they were tickled to death over the beard incident.

"I have to agree with little Marie," Agnes chuckled, dabbing a tear of mirth from the corner of her eye. "He did look a bit rough around the edges. It had to be much worse by the time he got home!"

Sitting on the edge of their seats throughout Faith's reading of the boat-capsizing story, the women were grateful to know it ended well, and with the happy news that Chuck would celebrate Thanksgiving in Elsie and Marie's home.

Faith folded the letter, and returned it to its envelope. "It's getting late. Are you up to hearing Elsie's news now, or should we wait until tomorrow?"

Elderly Sister Agnes firmly clasped her gnarled fingers together with an air of great anticipation. "No! I won't sleep a wink until I know what's going on with her and that film agent. Don't keep me in suspense!"

Sister Eymard, who was busy pressing autumn leaves and blossoms at her corner work table, looked up and enthusiastically agreed that Faith should proceed with the second letter.

The ladies were on needles and pins throughout Elsie's nerve-wracking description of Weston's attempted crime, but Harrison's heroic intervention made them clap and cheer.

"Glory be!" Agnes placed a trembling palm over her racing heart.

"God's hand was definitely upon our Elsie, as well as angels keeping watch. The Lord works in mysterious ways," Sister Eymard added with an expression of wonderment.

As hard as it was to read about Elsie making room in her heart for another man, they agreed it was only natural. During vespers, they prayed for blessings and guidance for the widow of their dear Jack O'Neill—sleeping somewhere in the fields of Flanders.

Moments before Wilma's violin recital, Elsie nervously hovered and paced in the wings, waiting for her daughter's turn. Pink-cheeked Maggie Rose Callahan was playing an Irish jig for her "Da" (a belated birthday gift). She'd worked long and hard to get it just right. Eddie Patrick Callahan beamed with pride, tapping his toes to the beat of his little *colleen's* solo.

Elsie frowned as she tugged on Wilma's elbow. "Stop nibbling your nails!"

"I can't help it, Mommy ... got butterflies in my tummy! Besides, didn't you say Auntie Marie *and* Daddy used to bite their nails, too? Musicians are *s'posed* to keep their nails short, you know!"

Elsie blew out an exasperated breath. "Oh Wilma! What am I to do with you?!" Straightening her daughter's hair bow, "You must look your best for *Twinkle, Twinkle Little Star*."

"Oh Mommy, I'm not playing *that* one! I picked my *favorite, Molly Malone!*"

Her mother gasped, recalling last night's dream. With a rush of emotion, Elsie bent over and gently patted her daughter on the heart. "You're Daddy's here," she whispered. "Make him proud!"

During Father Collins' Sunday sermon on Matthew 17:20, Suzanne Leach studied her best friend's hopeful smile and squeezed Marie's hand. She was proud of Marie in so many ways, admiring her playful zest for life and unwavering tenacity. She was a friend in the truest sense of the word (someone to be trusted who had never let her down). Marie's bold move to start her own, now flourishing, business was a stroke of genius, and unsubstantiated rumors were floating around town of a future Middleton School of Music. Marie's dream of a music career seemed to be coming true, after all.

As for her friend's obsession with Charles Hollister, Suzanne was impressed that Marie seemed more at peace than the day she'd poured out her heart in Tea Thyme, and was trusting in God for wisdom and guidance regarding her Cary (the perfect example of mustard seed faith). Suzanne still wasn't convinced they were right for each other, but she figured, *who am I to judge? I face enough challenges in my own search for a soul mate.* Lillian Bounds and Walter Disney were a different story. She thought them a perfect match and expected to hear wedding bells in the near future.

Marie's "Cary" seemed to keep her constantly spinning on an emotional roller coaster of which most women would quickly sicken, but not Marie! If anyone could crack the protective shell

Hollister seemed to have grown around his heart, her determined little friend could.

How delicious it was to encourage others to discover their God-given talents, and then sit back and watch while they reached their full potential (whether or not she approved of the course they chose to get there)!

Elsie dashed into Callahan's Monday evening, and quickly tied an apron around her middle.

"Sorry I'm a few minutes late. Marie's last student needed some extra pointers, and in light of the beach episode, I hesitated to leave the kids until she could give them her undivided attention." Scanning the diner, she spotted Stanley talking to a woman over bowls of Irish stew. Not *any* woman, but the kind and angelic Miss Winifred Britton, Wilma's second-grade teacher. *Odd*, she thought, since Stanley had no children. Something about the way they interacted with each other indicated they were more than casual acquaintances, and it bothered her. With relief, she noted that since Caty was their waitress she need not interrupt their dinner. Or so she thought, for Stanley had noticed her. With an exuberant smile, he stood, raised his lanky six-foot frame, and waved her over to their table. There was no escaping it, so she managed a nonchalant approach.

"Welcome to Callahan's, Miss Britton. I see you're both having Stanley's usual tonight."

"*My* usual, as well, Mrs. O'Neill. It's one of several things Stan and I have in common." Though Winifred's tone of voice bore no guile, Elsie's territorial instincts surfaced. *How silly of me*, she reprimanded herself. *He's bound to have other female friends—women who know him far better than I do.* She should at least take into consideration the fact that the honorable man had chosen to meet with another woman right under her nose, rather than appear to be sneaking around behind her back.

Stanley cut in with an explanation, "Winnie and I are on the Missions Committee at church, and planning our Thanksgiving Food Drive over dinner. Even in an affluent town like Coronado, we have families who could use a helping hand."

"What a wonderful thing to do! Yes, Sacred Heart *is* conducting a food drive. It's strange though, I haven't seen either one of you at Mass."

A surprised and slightly amused look passed between Stanley and Miss Britton before he responded with, "Well ... the thing of it is, Elsie ... we're not Catholic!"

The Middleton sisters poured over their guest list at the kitchen table. Time was running out to make their first Thanksgiving in California memorable. In the absence of immediate family, their newly *adopted* family would be invited—primarily those who might otherwise spend the holiday alone. Marie read the names, as Elsie placed check marks next to the responses. Suz, Mina, Mitzie and Paulo, Mrs. Gable, Stanley, and last but not least, Cary, were coming; the aunts were maybes, as well as a handful of friends from their parish. The Callahans were having their own huge clan reunion. Jonathan would have dinner with his family on the other side of the island, but promised to drop by later for pie. Reluctantly, Elsie had invited Winifred Britton, knowing she was fairly new to town with no family nearby. The thought of sharing

Stanley with her was not appealing, but including her daughter's teacher was the decent thing to do. Winnie's sweet disposition *would* make her a desirable addition to their group, and Wilma would be tickled pink. Finding out that Stanley wasn't Catholic had been a shock—something which should have crossed her mind, but hadn't. Should she even consider a future with someone outside of her faith? She must definitely pray about it, but what would Marie think?

Elsie had written to Mother, requesting her recipe for chestnut dressing and instructions for roasting a turkey. She was so afraid it would flop, but Mother had assured her it was fool-proof. Even though they'd told their guests not to bring a thing, most of them insisted on contributing specialty dishes.

The beach house would be cramped, but with clear skies predicted, they could set up tables in the back yard. Croquet and badminton would be available for their more sports-minded guests, and cards and checkers available for those who preferred a stationary form of gaming. An after-dinner stroll on the beach might appeal to others.

Marie had formed a plan to prolong her farewell to Cary as long as possible. If it worked, she'd tell him exactly how she felt before sending him off with a kiss to be remembered. Just thinking about it made her tingle!

Thanksgiving was shaping up to be a perfect day. For Marie, any day with Cary *was* a perfect day.

Chapter Thirteen

Marie hand shredded baguettes to the beat of "Doo Wacka Doo," the newly released fun and bouncy ragtime jazz song by the *Saint Louis Low Downs*. Before she knew it, she was doing the Charleston in the middle of the kitchen floor.

Bobby poked in his little blond head to see what the racket was all about. "Auntie Marie, you're funny!" Bobby giggled. She grabbed his hand and pulled him into the dance. They wildly moved their feet back and forth, kicked their legs and swung their arms—stopping only when the song did. Gasping for breath, Bobby squealed, "That was fun! Let's do it again!"

"Can't right now, Kiddo. Gotta make your grand-mère's stuffing for our Thanksgiving turkey. We'll do it again sometime real soon, okay?"

"It's a date!" Bobby bounded off through the hallway, and loudly announced to his sister, "Hey, Willie! Me and Auntie Marie just danced!"

Once the week's layer of dust was swept from the furnishings and floors, and grimy handprints were wiped off the door frames,

Elsie began watering her house plants. The Creeping Charlies were living up to their name; the entwining tendrils grew nearly an inch per week. Elsie emptied the last few drops from her watering can, remembering the very first Charlie she and Jack had received from Sister Faith. Its name was "Agnes," they'd been told, in honor of St. Agnes, and the motherly nun at Holy Infant. The name, which meant pure and holy, definitely fit the virtuous saint of old *and* the now retired Mother Superior at Orphanage of the Holy Infant. Her love, like the vines of this plant, was far reaching: weaving lives, hearts, and souls together in an intricate pattern, all for the glory of God. Elsie had started all of her Charlies from the original plant, and each one bore the name Agnes.

Elsie eagerly anticipated her approaching birthday dinner at a posh restaurant in San Diego with Stanley. Their relationship had moved to a higher level and she suspected he was working up to a proposal. They'd privately discussed their differences in faith—some more significant than others—and came to the conclusion that their feelings for each other were strong enough to surmount any obstacles placed before them. Faith in Christ was their common foundation. When she told Marie about her dilemma, her sister was cautiously supportive, saying that though she believed in the power of love, she feared there could be problems down the road. She hoped all would be well.

Elsie smiled wistfully as she plucked a withered leaf, and remembered the joyful days she, Jack, and newborn Wilma had shared in their tiny apartment before her husband was deployed. No, Stanley was not Jack, and his kisses didn't make her toes curl or bells ring like Jack's did; but Stanley was a kind and good man of high moral standing, with an uncanny sensitivity and respect for the feelings of others.

He was never unjust (being the first to recognize his own short-comings), and listened without reproach to the woes of those who found him to be a trusted confidante. With a passion for children, animals, and God, what more could she ask for? *Love?* She brushed aside her niggling conscience, and hoped it would come in time. For now, Elsie was quite fond of him, and must do what was best for Wilma and Bobby. The way Stanley looked at her made her feel like a movie star! Who needed Avery Weston with his shallow lifestyle and empty promises? She looked forward to their Thanksgiving celebration later today and the chance for Stanley and the children to get better acquainted. Until they learned to accept him, Elsie couldn't take the next big step.

Wilma reminded her aunt she hadn't followed through with the promise of a poetry lesson. Today was not the best time, thought Marie, but she couldn't find it in her heart to say no to Wilma's exuberance. The house was clean, the tables were set, and the meaty scent of the large, trussed bird roasting in the oven permeated every nook and cranny of the cozy bungalow. There was time to spare, so she sat the little redhead down at the kitchen table with a tablet of paper and a pencil. "First, you need to pick a topic. What do you want to write about, sweetie?"

Wilma rolled her eyes. "*Thanksgiving*, of course!"

Marie laughed at her slightly impudent niece. "Of course! Hmmmm, we need to make your first one simple. How about an acrostic?!"

"A what?"

Marie picked up the pencil and printed T-H-A-N-K-S-G-I-V-I-N-G vertically in large capital letters down the left margin of the page. "Take each letter and write a little sentence after it. Like 'A is for apple, B is for ball;' got it? Making the lines rhyme is fun, but they don't have to."

"Ooohhh!" Wilma clearly liked the idea. "I can do that!"

"All right, then. I'll leave you to your writing, and let me know if you need any help."

Marie had finished changing her clothes and arranging her hair when Wilma tapped on her bedroom door. "I'm all done, Auntie Marie!"

"My goodness, that was fast! May I see it?"

Wilma shyly held out the sheet of paper. "I hope you like it."

At first glance, Marie could see she had, indeed, filled every line of the acrostic in her child-like printing. She handed it back to the budding poet. "Here, Willie, you read it out loud to me. Hearing a story or poem read in the author's own voice is more meaningful."

Wide-eyed, Wilma took the paper from her hand, gulped, and began reading in a shaky voice. Her poem had captured the essence of the holiday—rich in tradition and appreciation for the good things in life. Wilma hung her head, with her signature self-conscious smirk.

The seven-year-old had by far exceeded Marie's expectations. "Willie, why do you look so embarrassed? It's great!"

Finally, Wilma raised her misty eyes to Marie's, "But you're so good, Auntie, and I never wrote a poem before. I thought it sounded stupid."

"I love it, and I want you to read it to our guests this afternoon!"

Wilma brightened and agreed to the recitation, but said she was nervous about having so many people looking at her. "Willie, it's no different than your violin recital. You'll be fine!"

The cheery little beach house hummed with activity: women shared recipes in the dining room, men smoked cigars and spun yarns on the front porch, while the younger set volleyed a birdie over the net stretched across the back yard. Everyone had clapped and cheered, "Brava! Brava!" when Wilma read her Thanksgiving poem prior to the blessing.

Elsie had moaned about her turkey not being as juicy as her mother's, but everyone else found it to be tasty; the chestnut dressing and rich gravy gave it a savory, pleasing flavor. The coolness of Mina's cucumbers drenched in sour cream was a nice compliment to the main dish, as well as Suzanne's "Orange Nummy" dish (Marie's name for it, after tasting her first heavenly mouthful of whipped gelatin and fruit). Mitzie took a stab at American cooking by providing a sweet potato casserole, which was a big hit. *Olé!* Once dinner settled, everyone anticipated large slices of Winnie's homemade apple pies and Aunt Madge's spicy pumpkin, topped with fluffy dollops of whipped cream. Madge had also surprised them by baking the raisin pie that Grandma Martha Middleton always made for Hugh's birthday.

So far, the day had been satisfying on every level.

Hues of indigo and amber painted the horizon as Charles and Marie wiggled bare toes in chilly rivulets along the shoreline. She ached for him to hold her hand, but he kept his own stuffed in his coat pocket. However, his unusually light-hearted mood bolstered her courage.

"I need to pick up some sheet music in the city tomorrow about the time your train leaves. Mind if I tag along to the depot and see you off?" Marie smiled expectantly into his raven eyes, waiting for his response. Happily, he agreed to her suggestion, and expressed how pleased he was with her offer. *So far so good,* she mused. *By this time tomorrow, he'll know what's in my heart and have my love to keep him warm as he sails across the Atlantic!*

As Harrison prepared to leave, Bobby hugged him about the knee and looked way up into Stanley's eyes. "I'm Mr. Bobby! You're da nice man who helped me build my sand castle, aren't ya? And ya gots a really big dog, too! I *like* dogs!" Then turning toward his mother, "Mommy, can we get a dog? Just like Becket?!" He flashed a scintillating smile which was always sure to melt her heart like butter and was too hard to resist (the one so like Jack's, it was uncanny). Elsie gently pried her son loose from Stanley's trouser leg and answered, "We'll see ... maybe someday." She shyly caught Stanley's eye.

Harrison fondly held her demure gaze while addressing the little tyke. "Maybe sooner than you think, Mr. Bobby."

Winnie Britton had witnessed the whole thing as she carried her nearly licked-clean pans from the kitchen. She lifted her hat and handbag from a hook on the hall tree, and graciously thanked her hostess before departing with a heavy heart ... feeling as empty as the pie tins.

Hollister had risen early to pack and review his itinerary. This year's Thanksgiving had been the best he could remember since his days at Holy Infant where the Sisters served a feast to be truly thankful for. Yesterday's "sisters" had equally outdone themselves. Yes, Elsie's bird came out a tad dry, but not bad for a first attempt; her fabulous gravy made up for it. Marie continued to astound him with her culinary skills. Anna Middleton would have been proud of Marie's chestnut stuffing: a mouthful of love!

Now that he and Marie were back on speaking terms, he could reevaluate his feelings for her. Marie's considerate suggestion to see him off at the depot had touched a place deep inside, opening a door which had been locked for many years. What he hadn't told her was that he never bothered to wait for someone to see him off, for no one ever came. He'd convinced himself long ago it was better that way. Now a glimmer of light gave him hope that circumstances were about to change in a way he hadn't let himself believe possible. What was it about Little Mimi that made *anything* seem possible?

Charles caught a whiff of Boise perfume and groaned. *Not today!* He tried to hide behind his newspaper, but there was no escaping her. Jayne had sniffed him out like a bloodhound and came sashaying over to his sun deck table. "Good morning, Darling! Where have you been hiding yourself? I thought for sure I'd see you in the Crown last evening for the big Thanksgiving spread, but you were nowhere to be found." Pouting her sculpted red lips, "It was dreadfully dull without you."

He smiled politely while folding up his paperwork and slipping it into his brief case. "I spent the holiday with my extended family, Jayne. I suppose I should have told you."

Jayne arched her eyebrows, "Extended family? I didn't know you had relatives in the area?" She indiscreetly peered at his documents. "And what have we here? Planning a trip? I hope not in the near future, Darling." Then, with an unmistakable gleam in her eye, "Not unless you take me along, that is!"

Being as vague as possible in response, "I do have some business to tend to, but if you care to join me for a few minutes, there's something I've been meaning to run by you."

She smiled expectantly as he pulled out her chair. "My, that sounds intriguing! Tell me every teeny, delicious detail!"

Charles pulled his billfold from his back pocket, and removed a folded sheet of paper from the currency compartment. "Jayne, you read French, don't you?"

"*Oui!* But of course, Charles! I studied at École des Beaux-Arts for a number of years in Pah-rié, and consider myself quite fluent! If you're planning to ask me what I *think* you are ... why, I'm getting goose bumps!" Miss Blackwell closed her eyes in ecstasy. "I can see us now in the City de L'amour! La Tour Eiffel, L'Arc de Triomphe, Notre Dame, Le Louvre ... "

Hollister chuckled at her theatrics. "Let's not get carried away, Jayne. That's not what I have in mind. However, this letter—possibly a poem—fell into my hands a while ago, and I'm wondering if you could translate it for me. You see, quite curiously, my name is at the top but I have no idea what it says. Would you mind?"

Her initial disappointment was overshadowed by natural curiosity. "*Mais oui bien sûr* (My pleasure)!" She reached for the paper with an alluring smile, "May I?"

Charles handed it over and waited several agonizing minutes as she silently read ... first with a smirk, then shock, and then a blank stare.

Too impatient to wait a second longer, Hollister broke into her contemplation. "Jayne, is something wrong? What does it say?"

She sighed and met his anxious gaze with pity in her eyes. "Well, Darling. I don't quite know how to tell you this. It seems someone (she knew precisely who) is telling you in no uncertain terms that they ... I assume it's a woman, based on the penmanship ... that *she* would rather be drowned in the depths of the sea than be loved by you! And, she's in love with someone else." With rising indignation, "What horrible person would write such a thing ... about *you* of all people? The finest, most eligible man in all of San Diego County! It's unconscionable!"

White as a sheet, Hollister could not believe his ears. Yes, Marie was known to joke around and it had crossed his mind that the letter might poke fun at him, but not something as hateful and mean-spirited as this. He thought she at least *liked* him. What had he done to deserve such scorn? Why had she continued to string him along, even though she'd rather die than be committed to him? And right when he thought they were back on track to a meaningful relationship. He'd noticed how Marie perked up when Jonathan Woods dropped by for dessert last evening. The two of them looked pretty cozy while laughing and joking around. They did have a lot in common with their closeness in age and love for music. The blow to his male ego was hard to take, but he couldn't let Jayne *or* Marie know how deeply wounded he was. He needed that devious blonde like a hole in the head! After all, Miss Marie Jeannette Middleton of Chicago wasn't the only pebble on the beach!

Jayne clutched the poem in both hands, intending to rip it to shreds. "Why don't you let me get rid of this piece of trash for you, Darling? It's definitely written by some deranged lunatic and not worth keeping."

Alarmed, Charles snatched it from her claws, accidentally tearing it in half. "Um, no, I think I'll hang onto it awhile, for laughs."

Jayne gasped, "I really think you're making a huge mistake!

Before saying goodbye, Hollister held Jayne's hands in his own and sincerely thanked her for translating the devastating poem. He leaned forward and kissed her on the cheek ... then softly on the lips. "I owe you, Jayne, and will be in touch."

Charles glanced at his wrist watch, knowing Marie would soon be waiting for him at the streetcar stop. Distasteful though it would be to travel with her to San Diego, he'd play dumb and feign indifference as he left town ... perhaps for good.

It seemed Jayne Blackwell was always on the losing end of love. She admitted to being controlling and overbearing, but she wasn't born that way. It was an acquired demeanor which came from being raised as the only child of overindulgent parents who pampered her and enabled her to be a spoiled brat. "You name it, I've got it," she'd tell potential playmates; but once they discovered she didn't know how to share, they'd drop her like a hot potato. *No, I've never learned to share, and I'm not about to start now!*

She'd collected men over the years like shiny beads on a string: visually appealing, but hollow inside. All they wanted was her money and other "assets." With Charles, she knew instantly he was not like the rest. He was the Real McCoy—a good and decent man of substance, with a heart. It had obviously been broken a time or two, but was still beating—in rhythm with her own, she hoped. At last, here was someone with the capacity to understand and care for her, having wounds akin to her own. For the first time in her life, there was a glimmer of hope to be loved and appreciated for who she was deep, down inside: a little girl needing a hug more than a new toy.

She saw how people tried to avoid her, the way Charles had unsuccessfully attempted to hide behind the business section of *The Sun* this morning. So transparent! She'd been forced to take the matter into her own hands, and it turned out better than if she'd planned it for weeks ... as long as he didn't wave that saccharine poem around. *If he shows it to someone who can reveal it's true meaning, my goose will be cooked!*

Something had changed since yesterday. Marie sensed it immediately on the streetcar and in the strained tension hanging heavily between them while crossing the bay by ferry. She'd hoped that he'd get over whatever was troubling him by the time they reached the city, but his sour mood remained unchanged. What had she done now?

The train's low-pitched whistle mournfully signaled the last call for boarding. They solemnly gazed at each other in silence. *Please don't let me cry*, Marie prayed. Mustering every ounce of courage she possessed, she offered him her trembling hand. "Well, I guess this is it." He held it a moment, studying her with a touch of despair in his soulful dark eyes (clouding her own). Marie's voice cracked. "You *do* know how I feel about you, don't you, Cary?"

His jaw muscles tightened. "I know *exactly* how you feel about me, Miss Middleton. Take care of yourself." After a strained pause, he cryptically added, "I could be gone a long time, so if there's something you need to do, don't let me hold you back."

Engulfed in sadness and confusion, she managed to murmur, "Bon Voyage, Cary."

He dropped her hand, turned and stepped into the coach, not once looking back. Marie choked on a sob; it sounded like he was saying "good-bye." With her hand held high in the autumn breeze, she unabashedly bawled, "Go with God, and come back to me, *mon amour!*"

Chapter Fourteen

In spite of emotional exhaustion, Marie knew she wouldn't sleep much that night. She sat on the front porch, bundled up in a wool blanket, with her journal clasped against her heart. The night was crisp and clear, nearly quiet enough to hear the distant breakers lick the shore. None of it made any sense. She and Cary had made progress, being able to speak to each other without some fiasco taking place. And to be able to smile and laugh together, rather than at each other, was nothing short of miraculous! How happy she'd been last night, when the fulfillment of her dream seemed within reach. Should she not have seen this coming, since her relationship with Cary had been plagued by emotional ups and downs?

This morning, Cary's sullen mood had returned, and for no fathomable reason. She must have unintentionally said or done something to throw him back into such a gloomy state ... even to the point of hinting she move on with her life without him. But what could it be?

Her head ached trying to sort it all out; the burning questions and speculations twisted and turned like Elsie's Creeping Charlie. Such a tangled web! It's what Mama would call *la douleur exquise* (the heart-wrenching pain of loving someone unattainable). Oh how she needed Mama's words of wisdom, which would likely be, "This, too, shall pass." Pops would probably say (in his teasing stab at humor): "Offer it up," or "Eat a banana. You'll feel better!"

Desperate to release her pent-up emotions, she poured them out through verse:

> They say if you love someone, set them free;
> And if they return, it was meant to be.
> He said au revoir, I felt like a fool.
> Tears threatened to fall, but I remained cool.
> Should I have cried and begged, "Cary, don't go!"
> Should I have blurted out, "I love you so!"
> Would he have mocked me and laughed, "Oh Marieee!"
> Or would he have promised never to leave?
> Words failed to come, and he's gone from my sight.
> It's too hard to tell if silence was right.
> If the man loves me, would not he say so?!
> Sometimes he seems to, but then ... I don't know.
> Though hoping seems futile, while we're apart,
> I'll pray he comes back, and brings me his heart.

She longed to be that carefree little girl who watched the world's woes play out from her oak tree balcony view. Pity, the only available tree at the moment was of the palm variety. She listened to its fronds scratching against each other in the darkness and whispered, "Come back to me, my darling."

Hollister stared blankly through the coach window as mile upon mile of heartland swept by. Part of him wished he'd taken the long way around by ship through the Panama Canal, but several colleagues awaited in New York, ready to sail for France. He definitely needed a vacation before long, but would take advantage of the next few days riding the rails to clear his brain and lick the wounds inflicted by his former fickle friend, Marie. A time of contemplation and soul searching wouldn't hurt.

Jayne Blackwell had her faults, but she made her intentions clear without playing mind games. Yes, she had a rather forward way of showing it, but at least she was upfront. Marie was an entirely different story: constantly leading him on an exhausting cat and mouse chase—as Elsie so aptly described it—which kept him guessing throughout the highs and lows, twists and turns.

He had half a mind to send for Jayne and take her on that "tour de Paris" she'd pinned her hopes on ... *until death do us part*. He suspected, like himself, she'd been shot down a few times in the romance department. Maybe they needed each other. His heart would be safe with Jayne, because she didn't have the power to break it. Once he was an old married man, he'd be off limits to anyone who could. Jayne was obviously in love with him, so maybe in time it would be enough for both of them.

He should have his head examined for keeping Marie's confounded scribbling! They were only words, but strong enough to shatter his heart. For some morbid reason, he'd tucked the hastily patched diatribe back into the darkest recesses of his wallet. *I'm getting too old for this*, he mused. Yet, there was no denying or escaping what he felt for Marie; and at long last, he ruefully confessed, *I'm in love with her!*

In the final weeks before Christmas, Wilma and Maggie Rose diligently rehearsed their duet for the school program: a simplified version of a newly published carol, *Ding Dong Merrily on High*. Though roughly four years apart in age, the girls had become good friends and were excited about playing the joyful little song together. It brought Marie back to the days at The Academy for Young Ladies in Aurora where she and Suz had performed several violin and piano duets. Mademoiselle Beaumont's decision to pair the girls as roommates was heaven-sent, and Marie hoped Wilma and Maggie would enjoy the same closeness through life as she and Suz had. Those spunky Irish lassies were quite a pair!

Jonathan Woods arrived at the end of the girls' practice session. Maggie whispered to Marie, "Caty has a crush on him, and I think he likes her, too, but he doesn't know it yet. Should I tell him?"

Maggie's words stung a little, even though Marie had seen it coming since her first date with Jonathan at Callahan's Café. With a heavy heart, she knew it was time to finally let him go ... along with Cary.

She smiled wistfully at Maggie and whispered in her ear, "I don't think so. It will be more fun to watch him figure it out on his own!" Then, Maggie Rose shyly confided that she also had a crush on someone. His name was Andrew Vincent, and he was the school's best trumpet player. She hoped *he'd* soon figure it out, as well! "My goodness, Maggie! At your age, I hated boys (*especially Cary*, she remembered). Don't be in a rush to grow up, sweetie. In a few years, boys will be buzzing around you like bees to honey!"

Stanley had barely touched his dinner. The only real appetite he had was for the ravishing brunette snuggled next to him on the front seat of his shiny black touring car—the woman who'd made him the happiest man on Earth! His beloved sighed contentedly and rested her head on his shoulder. Could she hear his heart nearly thumping out of his chest to beat the band? Her forehead fit perfectly into the contour below his cheek bone. He lightly brushed his lips against her hair, drinking in the scent of coconut oil shampoo and admiring of her newly bobbed hairdo. *Hotsy-totsy!* He'd been a wreck all through their meal, mentally rehearsing the speech he planned to give prior to dessert. He'd never forget the expression on Elsie's face when he knelt on one knee, holding out the black velvet ring box. She'd smiled confidently and joyfully, "Yes, Stanley! Of course I'll marry you!"

Stanley breathed a silent prayer of thanks to God for blessing him with this incredible woman. She'd been through a lot and her heart bore the scars of nearly fatal wounds, but she belonged to *him* now, and he'd do his best to make her happy. Over the age of thirty, he'd about given up on marriage and children, so the ready-made family was an added bonus. Wilma and Bobby were great kids, and he already felt fatherly and protective toward them. He'd been told stepparenting was usually an up-hill battle; but he was ready for the challenge, and prayed he'd be a good father and Godly role model for the two little rascals. He smiled optimistically, thinking he'd like to give them a few brothers and sisters, too!

The bungalow was ablaze with light when they pulled up to the curb. Obviously, Marie had gathered their friends together for a big birthday celebration. Wouldn't they be surprised to hear the news? Or, come to think of it, probably not so surprised, after all!

Stanley swelled with pride as Elsie's guests gaped in awe at the Royal Asscher cut diamond on her ring finger. He chuckled when Paddy called it a humdinger, but the ring didn't hold a candle to his beautiful fiancée! Of course, he'd asked Hugh Middleton for his blessing, but would have proposed with or without it. Elsie was all he'd ever wanted, and more.

Mitzie had baked her famous strawberry cream-filled cake, topped with pretty pink butter cream rosettes. Before blowing out her twenty-nine candles, Elsie'd beamed at him and said she didn't need to make a wish, since it had already come true. Even after the candles were extinguished, the room remained aglow from the radiance of his bride-to-be. The wedding would take place in mid-January. Yes, it was soon, but since the rest of the Middleton family couldn't come until the end of next year, the happy couple didn't want to wait. No time like the present, they figured. A simple church ceremony would suffice. Marie would, of course, be her maid of honor, and he had chosen Paulo for his best man. Naturally, Wilma and Bobby would round out the bridal party as flower girl and ring bearer. From the way Paddy Callahan was blubbering, it was evident Elsie had asked him to give her away in the absence of her dad.

Stanley Harrison, Coronado's Town Hero and upstanding citizen, was to be lauded once again. No medal of honor could outshine the dazzling jewel this night had awarded: Elsie Josephine O'Neill!

He was positively euphoric: bathed in a pool of light, eyes glistening with tears, and shouting, "I remember you!"

Elsie awoke, sensing Jack was trying to tell her something. But what? And why the ridiculous proclamation in her dream? *Of course you remember me, Jack! Soul mates don't forget!* Then it dawned on her that he thought *she* had forgotten *him.* Never! "I'll love you forever, my darling, no matter what." The ceiling danced with reflected sparkles from the multi-faceted rock on her finger, as she rubbed sleep from her eyes. Last night had far exceeded her expectations. Yes, she'd suspected Stanley would propose, but the joyous reactions of her family and friends confirmed she'd made the right decision. Wilma and Bobby jumped up and down with excitement upon learning they would finally have a Daddy, and a dog!

Paddy often tried to hide his big, soft heart; but when she asked him to give her away, he made no bones about showing his emotion. Of course, that right belonged to Father, but he was 2,000 miles away, and Mr. Callahan treated her like one of his own. He'd even closed the diner early last night to attend her birthday party—a rarity.

In spite of Marie's exuberance, something was off. Elsie needed to have another heart-to-heart with her sister sometime soon.

Mitz had outdone herself with the beautiful birthday cake; and Paddy was strongly considering the addition of a bakery counter in the diner, featuring Mitzie's creations which often included some form of strawberry this or that.

Only one person stood out as not sharing in their joy. Actually, she didn't stand out at all, but retreated to a gloomy corner before eventually slipping away unnoticed by everyone but Elsie. Winnie's sad countenance tugged at her conflicted heart. "She loves him more than I do. But *he* loves *me*! The words Shakespeare had written for Polonius, which Marie sometimes quoted, flashed through Elsie's mind with a stab of guilt. *This above all: to thine own self be true ... Thou canst not then be false to any man.* If she remained true to herself and to Jack, she'd be single the rest of her life, ending up a cloistered old widow with a house full of cats after the children had grown up and away. Right now, they needed a father, and she needed someone to fill the cavernous void in her life— someone to grow old with. Seeing aging couples walk hand-in-hand, smiling tenderly into each other's eyes, made her insanely jealous. Oh, how she longed for it! Stanley was such a dear, and she considered herself lucky to have him. However, was she marrying him for the wrong reasons, knowing someone else wanted him for all the right ones?

From her bedroom window, Marie watched Elsie and the children scurry down the chrysanthemum-lined walkway. She was sincerely happy for her big sister. Elsie deserved a good man like Stanley, and they were few and far between ... or far away. She tried to picture Cary on his long journey to Paris, berating herself for not being more open with him about her feelings. She talked bravely when he wasn't around: "if he stomps off again, I'll stomp right behind him;" but when the most crucial moment arrived, she was tongue-tied and frozen in place by the finality in his eyes and voice. So many questions. With or without Cary, she prayed one day she'd have the answers.

For now, there were more pressing matters to consider. *Once Elsie is married, what will become of me?* With Stanley's substantial income, Elsie would no longer have to work two jobs, if at all, and Marie would no longer be needed. It wouldn't be appropriate to live under the same roof as the newlyweds; they needed to establish their marriage in private. She thought they were rushing it a bit, with the wedding a little over a month away, but they did seem to belong together.

Although her clientele was picking up, Marie wasn't making nearly enough to rent even a small room for herself. There was only one logical plan of action. *My work here is done. It's time to return to Chicago and the Music Conservatory. I'll write to Mama and Pops and make arrangements to leave Coronado right after Elsie's honeymoon. I'm going home!*

As much as she'd miss her life and friends in Coronado, she was content with her decision. She spoke aloud with confidence, "The God who brought me here is the same God who will guide me the rest of the way."

What is it Mama says about the lilies? She reached for her white Douay-Rheims Bible (the one she'd been given by her godparents as a confirmation gift), and opened it to the place she'd marked before leaving Chicago. There it was, in the sixth chapter of Matthew, where Jesus told his disciples not to worry about food, drink, clothing, or even life itself. For if our Heavenly Father can dress the lilies in beautiful raiment, clothe the fields with grass and provide food and rest for the birds of the air, surely He will do the same for His children. *O ye of little faith!*

Bowing her head, she breathed her standard morning offering, "I do not know what will happen to me today. I only know that nothing will happen that was not foreseen by You, and directed to my greater good from all eternity. I adore Your holy and unfathomable plans, and submit to them with all my heart. Amen."

It was their turn to close after a busier than usual Friday, having locked up early last night for Elsie's memorable party. With aching backs and feet, Caty and Maritza had stacked chairs on top of tables before pushing their wet rag mops over the diner's floor. Their hands were chapped from scrubbing surfaces with harsh cleaning products.

This diner was Caty's second home. Ma'am and Da had originally opened Callahan's as a street-corner stand, selling their homemade corned beef sandwiches when she was ten years old. New to America, Eddie Patrick and his wife, Maureen, struggled to learn the language and culture, and worked hard to blend into the big "melting pot." Expecting handouts or special compensations was as foreign to their Irish heritage and pride as they were to the strange and captivating new land of perpetual sunshine and swaying palms. They'd come a long way in the past fifteen years, and Caty was proud of them.

She longed for the day when she would have her own help-mate by her side to face life's challenges and accomplishments. After Jonathan Woods left for college, she'd been asked out by other young men, but her heart wasn't in it.

Da's right, she thought, *I've been pinin' away fer him.*

She'd waited so long for Jonathan's inevitable return to Coronado. Now that he seemed to be back for good, they'd barely said more than few a words to each other, smitten as he was with his beguilin' teacher whom he'd stuck to like glue at the party last night. She didn't stand a chance against the younger, beautiful, and cultured Marie Middleton.

Caty brushed back a stray, brown wisp which had come loose from her Celtic knot, and looked over at Mitzie. "What'd ya think o' Elsie's engagement ring? Wasn't it grand?!"

"*Si, grande* (large)! *Muy bonita* (very pretty)! Fat chance Paulo will be able to afford one like that for me, if he ever gets around to popping the question. But I love him so much, I'd be happy with a cigar band!" She dreamily stared into thin air, and sighed. "My Paolo's the cat's meow, but he keeps dragging his feet."

Caty sighed. "Why aire fellers so thick headed?"

Mitzie dipped her mop into the scrub bucket and paused before squeezing out the excess water. "It's Señor Jonathan, isn't it? I see how you look at him and how red your face gets whenever he's around."

With an even deeper sigh, "Aye, there's no hidin' it, 'tis there? Alas, what am I to do?"

Mitzie stepped over to Caty and hugged her. "Don't worry, Amiga. I happen to have some inside information about that one. Marie is definitely not in love with Jonathan. Give him time, and he'll be looking for someone else; there's a good chance it will be you!"

"Wha' if he still won't gi' me a whirl?"

"If not, then he really *is cabezon* (thick headed)!"

Chapter Fifteen

It had rained for days. Not nonstop, and not quite the proverbial cats and dogs, but enough to deeply soak the parched landscape. The steadiest torrents provided a good overdue washing of dirt and grime from vegetation and walkways, leaving a fresh, earthy scent in their wake. Between showers, bevies of thrashers, swallows and jays emerged from their hiding places, chirping and fluttering about in search of juicy earthworms and snails before the next downpour; provided the more aggressive crows and gulls didn't beat them to it.

Wilma gingerly stepped around the deeper puddles, but her little brother energetically sloshed right through them, splashing water over the tops of his rubber galoshes and onto his persnickety sister's over-the-knee white stockings. "Bobby O'Neill! You're getting me all wet!"

"Aw, p . . ., I mean, fiddlesticks! A little water won't hurt ya none, and it's fun!"

"You're right, Bobby it *is* fun, but you don't want to spend all morning at school with soggy feet, do you?" his aunt gently corrected him. "Walk like a gentleman the rest of the way, and after

school, you can get as wet as you please. In fact, I just might splash in the puddles with you!"

Wilma was aghast! "*Ladies* don't do that! Only *tomboys*!"

Guilty as charged, Marie confessed, "So I've been told!"

Bobby behaved himself the rest of the way, but eyed the puddles as he followed his sister around them. Between hugs at the school gate, Wilma announced her class would be making beauuu-tee-ful paper snowflakes today. Not to be outdone, Bobby chimed in that Miss Patty's kindergarten class would be creating colorful paper chains to string around the classroom. Marie's suggestion to make some of each for their own home was met with enthusiastic smiles and nods. It would break her heart to leave the children, but life was changing for all of them. *To everything there is a season.*

With Christmas less than two weeks away, Marie walked downtown to finish her gift shopping. Fresh pine wreaths trimmed with large red bows adorned every lamp post, and most of the store windows featured Christmassy displays with frosty snow scenes and holly leaves painted on the glass. It was like stepping into a Currier & Ives lithograph. Strains of traditional Christmas carols trickled through doorways as Marie window shopped.

The kids had been starry-eyed while watching the Christmas Parade along Orange Avenue on Saturday night, and the family looked forward to Christmas Eve when they would attend Midnight Mass following the annual lighting of The Del's living Christmas tree. It was said to be at least 50 feet tall, and the world's first outdoor tree ever to be illuminated with electric lights.

On her last trip to the city (the depressing farewell at the depot), Marie had picked up cakes of rosin to give each of her students, as well as packets of new strings. She'd ordered something frilly from Middleton Clothiers for Elsie's trousseau (due to arrive next week in the same shipment as the wedding gown). Mama and Pops had insisted on making that contribution to the wedding, since they couldn't be there in person. Elsie wanted an embroidered blue and white knee-length tulle that she'd seen in a *Vogue Magazine*, but they told her she'd have to wait and be surprised. Aside from that, their parents hinted at having something else up their sleeves. For herself, Marie needed to find a dress suitable for her role as maid of honor. Elsie said it could be any style she preferred, as long as it was royal blue.

Marie needed to pick up some painting supplies for Suz, a pair of flashy earrings for Auntie Madge, and a little toy or two for each of the kids. She'd already mailed packages home to her family members in Chicago, she'd give Tante Arletta a dainty demitasse set for her collection. That pretty much summed up her shopping list.

One name was conspicuously missing, she noted with a wave of sadness. She wondered how *he* would celebrate the holidays, if at all. Christmas was no time to be away from loved ones, and certainly not to be spent on the other side of the world! She envisioned him dismally dining on roast goose with prunes at a table for one in a little Parisian bistro.

Something caught her eye in the haberdashery window. "Why not? I've got nothing to lose."

Days flew by, and it was time for the elementary school's Christmas program. Effervescent Cora Michaels, Principal, welcomed her guests with a cheery "Merry Christmas!" before leading them in the Pledge of Allegiance. Grandmotherly Miss Patty's kindergarten class was first on the program. Bobby sang his heart out wearing a Santa cap for *Jingle Bells*, and replaced it with a sparkly halo for *Hark, the Herald Angels Sing*. The program concluded with Maggie Rose and Wilma's beautiful violin duet, *Ding Dong Merrily on High*. Wilma winced a time or two at her sour notes, but Elsie beamed with pride. Miss Britton noticed how Maggie Rose blushed when Andrew Vincent smiled approvingly from the audience. The crowd sang in unison, "We Wish You a Merry Christmas," before filling up on festive homemade cookies and wassail.

Winifred watched with a stab of envy as the merry O'Neill group piled into Stan's automobile. She'd learned at an early age that she had the gift of reading the color of people's hearts. *His is gold* (priceless) *and hers is purple* (nostalgic and sad ... like her own at the moment). She wanted the very best for them, and offered a sacrificial prayer of blessing for their upcoming nuptials. Pulling her wrap more snugly about her, she braced herself for a cold and lonely Christmas.

The future Mrs. Harrison kissed her tuckered out babies goodnight, pulling the warm covers over their soft little shoulders. How blessed she was to have these two and a man who would love and care for them. Christmases had been difficult since Jack passed on. Each year she'd plastered on a cheery smile for the kids' sake, but had always been glad when the day was over.

Her thoughts turned to Jack's family (the Sisters in Oak Park). She'd sent them each a little something: a tin of her homemade fudge for Sister Agnes's sweet tooth; a collection of color postcards from the Botanical Building at Balboa Park for Sister Eymard; and a first edition copy of *Lad a Dog* for Sister Faith, knowing her fondness for furry friends (particularly Chihuahuas and Labs). She'd included a long letter, telling them about Stanley, and prayed they'd be happy for her. Smiling as she slipped into her cozy flannel nightgown, Elsie realized for the first time in years, that she didn't dread Christmas.

December 20th, the Saturday before Christmas, brought another cloudburst. Marie glumly sipped her morning tea by the kitchen window, watching rain fill the cupped leaves of the Bird of Paradise and then drip, drip, drip onto the pavers below. The children's homemade snowflakes and paper garlands were strung about the house, fresh greenery and holly draped the mantle, but the spot where the Christmas tree should stand was empty. Since she felt as gloomy as the weather, and Elsie was preoccupied with wedding plans, they hadn't made time for it. Whipping up her favorite cake recipe—the one Mama had found in *The Saturday Evening Post*—should lift her spirits. *If chocolate doesn't do the trick, what will?*

A pounding on the front door startled Elsie, who was scrubbing mud from Wilma's white socks in the bathroom sink. She quickly dried her hands on a terrycloth towel and headed for the door, with her curious little ones right behind her.

"Who's there?"

A man's deep voice answered, "Ho, Ho, Ho!! Merry Christmas!"

"What in the world?" Elsie cautiously opened the door, and was astonished to see a large, pungent-scented pine tree. The children giggled with delight as the grinning mystery man poked his red-capped head around the upper boughs.

"Stanley! A Christmas tree for *us,* and in this weather?! You dear man!" Elsie was clearly overcome.

Leaning the evergreen against the doorframe, Stanley brought in a stand, a galvanized bucket, and a box filled with colorful strings of lights. While he worked at securing the tree trunk in the stand before dropping it into the water bucket, Elsie fashioned a star from a tinfoil-covered piece of stiff corrugated paper. Marie busied herself by showing the children how to make popcorn and cranberry garlands. When the job was done, Stanley plugged in the lights, instantly transforming the dreary parlor into a magical fairyland.

"Ooops! We forgot something," Elsie said, handing the star to Stanley.

He could easily have attached it to the treetop himself, but paused to look down at Bobby. His voice was thick with emotion, "I'm not the man of the house yet, and this honor belongs to Mr. Bobby." Lifting him onto his shoulders, he let the proud little fellow set the star in place.

Stanley pulled a flat item from the bottom of his box and walked over to the Victrola. Gazing at the glowing pine, the family's hearts overflowed with joy as the German Carl Nebe quartet sang "O Tannenbaum."

Elsie dabbed unexpected tears with the corner of her kitchen apron. *Can it be? Am I actually falling in love?* After all, Christmas *was* the time of miracles.

Tying a bow around the flat, narrow package containing a scarlet necktie, Marie second-guessed her purchase. *It won't be opened this Christmas, but next year...?* She tenderly caressed the tag bearing his name, the one she alone hailed him by, "Cary." *No point in putting it under the tree*, so she gently laid it inside her cedar chest. Somehow, the comfort of knowing it was there gave her hope. "Joyeux Noël (Merry Christmas), mon amour."

Elsie had picked up an extra-large roast and a ten-pound sack of russets for tomorrow's Christmas dinner, anticipating easy meals from the leftovers during the busy week to follow. After putting away the groceries, she'd popped a batch of cookies in the oven. While they baked, she added more kindling to the fireplace and anxiously peered through the steamy parlor window. No sign yet of the mail truck bearing the box with her wedding gown. In Mother's most recent "Dear All" letter, she'd been assured it would arrive "any day now." With the wedding only three weeks away, she fretted over the possible need for alterations. It could take time.

Startled by the buzzing of the stovetop timer, Elsie stepped away from the window and scurried to the kitchen. "Hope they didn't burn!" She turned off the timer, grabbed the potholders, and pulled the tray of light golden sugar cookies from the hot belly of the oven, just in time. Once they cooled, the kids would have fun decorating them; the project would be a good way to distract them from shaking those intriguing packages under the Christmas tree.

The rumble of a motor put a smile on her face. "It's here!" Racing to the front door and jerking it open, she was dismayed to see not the mail carrier at all, but a taxi; its driver unloaded bags and boxes onto her front walk. "What in the world?" Then a tiny middle-aged woman with a salt and pepper bun emerged from the back seat. "Stars and garters! It's Nanette LaNell!"

"Joyeux Noël!" Father's cheerful lead seamstress called out a greeting as she struggled with some bulky parcels. Well over fifty, she still looked and acted like a young girl.

Elsie hurried to her side, taking a large clothing box from her hand. She could not believe her eyes, wondering if she'd missed the letter announcing her visit. "Merry Christmas! What a wonderful surprise, Nanette! It's so good to see you!"

"Sorry to drop in on you like this on Christmas Eve, *Chérie*, but Hugh and Anna insisted I come and deliver your wedding gown in person!"

Elsie stared at the box in her hands. "It's in *here*? My dress?!"

Nanette nodded, squinting at Elsie through spectacles perched on her nose tip. "Hmmm ... my sewing box will definitely be put to good use, cutting the garment down a smidgeon here and there. *Vous êtes mince* (you're thin)!"

"I've been too excited to eat much lately, Nanette, and nearly worried myself to death wondering if my dress would get here on time."

With her cute little giggle which Elsie so well remembered, Miss LaNelle assured her, "Lay your worries to rest, *Chérie*, Nanette's here!"

⚜

The chapel bells chimed *Silent Night* as they reverently stood before the nativity scene on the grounds of Sacred Heart Church—a quick stop before heading to The Del for the tree-lighting ceremony. Wilma shivered in the crisp night air, begging to leave, but Bobby wouldn't budge as he stared at the carved infant lying in the manger. "Mommy, where did Baby Jesus come from?" Elsie gave Stanley a nod, directing him to take Wilma back to the car.

Placing a gloved hand on her son's shoulder, "Bobby, God sent His only son to Earth from Heaven a long, long time ago, so He could save us from our sins. You remember the Easter story, don't you, about how Jesus died on the cross and then rose from the grave?"

"Uh huh," Bobby nodded, still staring at the Holy Child. "But I don't unnerstan all of it." He paused and sucked in a breath of chilly air before asking, "Mommy, did you get me from a cabbage patch?"

His perplexed mother asked, "What on Earth would give you an idea like that?"

"Well, some kids at school said I don't look like you or Willie, so you must've found me in a cabbage patch. Did ya?"

Her heart nearly stopped, realizing the time she'd dreaded had already come. *But why now, Lord? Why on Christmas Eve?* she inwardly groaned. *He's still a baby!* A voice deep within her spirit answered, *He's asking. What better time than now to give him the gift of truth? Trust me.*

With a pounding, aching heart, she said, "No, Bobby. Not a cabbage patch. However, I did get you from a very nice lady who asked me to be your Mommy, because she couldn't take care of you herself."

Bobby tore his gaze away from the crèche and glared at her in disbelief with imploring blue eyes. "Ya mean, you're not my *for realz* mommy? I gots a nudder one some'eres?" Then bursting into tears, his voice filled with hurt and despair, "Why didn't *she* want me? Didn't she love me?"

Elsie crouched down and wrapped her arms gently around his heaving shoulders. "In her heart, she did want you very much, honey, but she couldn't keep you. She was afraid bad things would happen if she did. It's sort of like the story of Baby Jesus. Mary was a pure-hearted, humble and obedient girl who God the Father chose to be the mother of his Son, so Jesus could grow up on Earth among us and show us how to know and love God. After Jesus died on the cross, Mary cried when she lost her son, like your birth mommy did when she gave you to me. Jesus gave His life to save us from sin, and your birth mother gave you up to save you from sadness. It's called being adopted, and has everything to do with love. I can't explain it all to you very well, right now, but when you're a little older I will. And if you want me to, one day I'll help you find her." (Had she really just said that?) "For now, please believe she loves you and prays for you every day and didn't throw you away. She chose me to be your mommy because she knew I would love you like she did and keep you safe. So you see, Bobby, you're a very special boy, because you have *two* mommies who love you with all their hearts."

Still racked with sobs as he wiped his runny nose on a coat sleeve, Bobby spoke with a trembling voice, "I don't need a nudder mommy. I gots *you!*" Then shuddering in fear, "You're not gonna gimme *back*, are ya?"

Elsie could stand it no longer and bawled like a baby. "Of course not, honey! You're *my* little boy, for keeps!"

"Cross your heart?"

"Cross my heart!"

A cheer arose from the crowd, breaking the hushed silence. A towering Norfolk Island Pine lit up the night with hundreds of red, yellow, blue, and green bulbs; while voices, young and old, united in song. "Joy to the World! The Lord is come ..."

Elsie was sandwiched between her men—Stanley to the left with his strong arm wrapped around her shoulders, and Bobby gripping her right hand for dear life. *The poor little guy*, she thought with a heavy heart. *He's obviously traumatized now that he knows he's adopted.* She prayed silently for his troubled little heart to find enough assurance to believe that like the Savior whose birth they celebrated, she would never leave him or forsake him.

She was back home, blissfully scribbling poetry in the shade of the old oak tree. A rustle above diverted her attention. Thinking it was Martha's cat, Sneakers, Marie pushed herself to her feet as he swung into view. Cary dangled by his knees, grinning like the Cheshire Cat, and waved a sheet of paper above her head. Not *any* paper, but her *poem*—her *French* poem! "Bonjour, Mademoiselle," he greeted her with a mocking laugh. Stretching to grab the sheet of paper, she toppled over. Rubbing her sore forehead, she opened bleary eyes to find herself lying on the hardwood floor at the side of her bed. "That exasperating man! I *knew* it was him the whole time!"

Elsie stuffed scraps of wrapping paper, ribbons, and bows into a corrugated paper carton (the aftermath of their frenzied

Christmas morning gift opening). It seems the simplest gifts are the best, which was proven by the little treasures Wilma and Bobby received by mail from the Sisters.

Nostalgically, Bobby had been sent a toy belonging to his daddy: a wooden acrobat flip toy with a little monkey which turned summersaults when the sticks were squeezed together. It had been handmade by a dear, elderly farmer (now gone on to Glory), Roy Lester ... better known to all the children as "Grampa Roy." He'd loved making toys as much as the children loved receiving them, but they had loved *him* even more.

For Wilma, there were a few little holy cards made from old greeting card pictures glued to lace edges, which she proudly hung on the Christmas tree.

The Sisters had tucked in a Christ candle for Elsie, also covered with a beautiful Nativity scene. It was to be lit on Christmas, as a symbol of The Light of the World, and at every Sunday dinner throughout the year, as a reminder to keep their own lights shining in preparation for Christ's return.

"It's such a treat to have you here for Christmas morning, Nanette! Your French croissants are as light as feathers, and better than ever!"

"*Merci*, Elsie! I love the silver sewing thimble pendant you gave me. It's *tres charmant* (very charming) and looks beautiful against my burgundy crepe de chin dress, don't you think? When did you find time to buy it?"

"Since you asked, Nanette, I raced to the jeweler's yesterday, just before closing time. I'm so glad you like it, but what really sets off your dress is the handmade Alençon lace collar. You do such beautiful work. I'd never be able to make lace."

Nanette smiled wistfully. "Elise, we all have our own talents, and yours is being a good mother. That's one of life's joys that I missed out on, since I never married. But look at you with two beautiful children and a wonderful man to share your life with!" Elsie hugged her dear friend. "Those words are the best gift I received today. "Joyeux Noël, Nanette!"

Moments after Tante Arletta's arrival, the doorbell rang again. There stood Maritza and Paolo, brimming over with Christmas joy. "Feliz Navidad! Sorry to barge in on you," Mitzie apologized, "but I have to show off my Christmas gift from Paolo!" She held out a small box containing a cigar band, and got a kick out of Elsie's mystified expression. "*Muy lindo* (Very nice), *Si*?! Just what I asked Santa for!" Then, with a huge grin, she pulled her left hand out of her coat pocket and flashed a round solitaire in a plain gold setting!

"Mitzie! Paolo! You're engaged!!! Congratulations!! Merry Christmas!" The two women hugged each other with squeals and tears of joy; simultaneously, Stanley smiled and patted Paolo on the back. "Well done, *mi amigo*, well done!"

Paolo grinned from ear to ear. "I'll have to work overtime at the construction site to pay for it, but my Mitzie's worth every penny and more!"

The way the house was filling up, Elsie was thankful for the enormous roast she'd had the foresight to buy. There'd be no leftovers this week, but they wouldn't starve to death.

Marie occupied herself by sweeping up pine needles from behind the Christmas tree, shielding herself from the gaiety around her. She paused and frowned, touching the sore spot on her forehead, remembering the one who'd caused it. Yesterday she'd received a festive card from her former beau, Bradley Smythe, with an enclosed note saying he was in a serious relationship. Marie indulged herself in a moment of self-pity, thinking that everyone's Christmas wish had come true but hers.

Before turning in for the night, Marie reflected on all that had taken place during the past few days, berating herself for her lack of faith. Although signs of God's love and grace were all around, she'd missed them. Worst of all, she'd overlooked what this beautiful holiday was all about: not what she wanted and didn't get, but what she'd already been given nearly 2,000 years ago. She ripped up what she'd begun to write, and started over:

A little bit of Heaven came down to us that day.

The Babe, only a hint of God's eternal love;

The star, just a glimmer of its brilliant source;

Angelic voices, an echo of celestial joy.

To witness God's full glory

Would have blinded mortal eyes,

And caused men's hearts to fail.

So a little bit of Heaven came down to us that day;

A Baby we could all embrace,

To make us holy unto God.

Chapter Sixteen

December 26, 1924

An extraordinary turn of events had curtailed Hollister's business trip weeks ahead of schedule. His most far-fetched dreams would not have given an inkling of what awaited him in Paris. He'd arrived on Sunday, December seventh, and spent a week attending fashion exhibitions to bone up on the latest trends in men's wear for the Heroes' Haberdashery project to benefit wounded American war heroes. When one of his colleagues became acutely ill with appendicitis, Charles escorted him to the American Hospital of Paris where Hollister discovered the surprise of his life.

Charles watched his companion snoozing in a chair, and smiled. He peeked through the porthole toward the western horizon, and willed the ship to glide faster and faster over the churning waters of the Atlantic. Before nightfall, the Statue of Liberty would be in sight. He decided to follow his companion's example and stretched out on the bed, but remained wide awake while the incredible details of the past two weeks replayed through his mind.

⚜

The frigid breeze across the Seine had caused him to shiver ...
even under a heavy wool overcoat. After he'd rounded the corner
onto rue Chauveau, his heart had missed a beat at the sight of a
young woman with sandy ringlets. She had shot a wary glance at
his half-raised arm. Flooded with embarrassment, he'd politely
tipped his hat, jammed the impulsive hand into his coat pocket,
and pushed on against the wind.

I have to forget her, he berated himself, *but she pops up at every
corner!* Of all the willing, eligible females he'd met, why on Earth
did he have to go and fall for the least interested: *the little minx who
made it her mission to play me for a fool ... the one who'd rather be
drowned in the depths of the sea?* Which of her devious little spells
had done the trick: her heart-stopping, death-defying acrobatic
stunts; her seductive glide down the stairway; or, was it merely those
mesmerizing baby blues? Somewhere along the line she'd bewitched
him. *Blast!*

He'd turned in at #44 rue Chauveau for a repeat visit to his
ailing colleague. The American Hospital of Paris appeared to be another casualty of war (in need of refurbishing after treating countless
wounded soldiers), but it was the best option available to American
citizens in France.

Passing the reception desk, there it was again: the haunting
whistle he'd heard yesterday, but had been unable to trace. Tempted
to follow the sound, he thought better of it since his colleague
awaited him in the opposite wing.

Just before leaving the facility, he'd stopped in his tracks. The
confounded whistling had resumed, this time louder and clearer.
Some sort of an Irish tune, maybe? He found it mystifying. There was
no getting around it—he could no longer resist the magnetic draw

of the whistle's call. Following his instincts, he'd turned toward the recreation room where he saw "Mr. Whistler," sitting with his back to the door in a wheelchair, entertaining one of the nurses with his repertoire of Irish melodies.

At the sound of footsteps, the nurse had smiled and asked if he needed assistance. He explained that he'd been enticed by the entrancing song of the Pied Piper. The nurse laughed at the analogy, coming closer to Hollister. She held out her hand, and introduced herself.

"I'm Babette Willette, a physical therapist assigned to this patient's case."

"Nice to meet you, Madame Willette. I'm Charles Hollister, here on business from the States to initiate a special project for disabled vets. Can you tell me anything about your patient?"

"I don't think he would mind if I give you some background, Mr. Hollister. We call him John. He's an American veteran who suffered multiple injuries, including severe brain trauma, when his Nieuport fighter was shot down by a German Zeppelin over Flanders. His earliest prognosis was grave. He slowly recovered from the life-threatening injuries, but continued to experience full loss of speech and memory. The first oral skill to return was his ability to whistle. A strange phenomena, indeed, but somehow the whistling miraculously led to further healing. After a long, hard battle, he's scheduled for release and return to the states within days."

"He just might be the first American vet to benefit from Hero's Haberdashery. May I talk to him?"

Babette encouraged him to do so. She'd walked over to John and whispered something to him, at which he nodded yes. Babette gave Charles permission to approach her patient, and excused herself with a sweet smile.

Hollister had cleared his throat before saying, "Excuse me, sir. I understand you're an American hero. Would you mind talking to someone from home? I'd consider it a great honor."

John turned slightly toward Charles, "That would be swell! Please join me," he'd cordially replied.

Seeing the man's profile and hearing his voice, Hollister had nearly passed out. *Can it be?* Moving to the front of the man's wheelchair and looking him squarely in the eye, there was no doubt about it. "Mr. John Whistler" was none other than the living, breathing Jack O'Neill!

"Jack! It's me ... *Chuck!* Do you know me?"

It had taken Jack a few seconds, but once he'd recognized his old pal, he burst into tears.

"Chuck! Is it really you?" The men embraced, having a hard time believing it wasn't just a wonderful dream.

They had a million questions for each other, and the mystery of Jack's disappearance and presumed demise began to unravel.

"This place has me listed as a John Doe, but my memory came back quite recently." Jack glanced over his shoulder. "They don't know it yet. I need to remain incognito a while longer."

Charles was flabbergasted, "Why on earth haven't you told them, Jack? And better yet, why haven't you contacted Elsie?"

"Chuck, when I go home, to my family, I want to be a whole man, not one to be pitied. Jo Jo deserves someone strong and healthy enough to provide for her and little Wilma, and possibly more children down the road. I just graduated to walking a few steps with a cane, but that's not enough. I want to *run* to her arms!"

When Charles told him Elsie had a son and was living in San Diego, Jack had replied with a look of despair, "Just what I feared. It's too late ... she's married."

Charles explained that Bobby had been adopted after the war, but that Elsie wasn't remarried. "Not yet." He told him about Stanley Harrison, "He's a top-notch guy. You'd like him, Jack, but Elsie has never stopped loving you. She's had a rough go of it, and you'd be real proud of her. She's a courageous young woman, but longs to share her life with a man who will be a good to her and the kids. From what I saw on Thanksgiving, she and Harrison are getting serious. You can't let her marry another man when you're still alive! Don't be a fool! Swallow your pride! Knowing Elsie like I do, she'll take you back in a heartbeat ... with or without legs!"

Jack's chin had quivered in a wave of emotion. After regaining his composure, Jack had told his story, filling in the gap of the past seven years.

Though presumed dead by allied troops on the ground, Jack had miraculously survived the crash that horrific day in early November, 1917. Found alive by the Germans, he was taken captive and detained in a prison infirmary for a full year. At the end of the war, he was handed over to the allies and temporarily admitted to a military hospital in Belgium. Having been stripped of his uniform by the enemy, and unable to speak, there was no way to identify him or pinpoint his national origin.

In the spring of 1919, a grieving couple came in search of their lost son, hoping against hope they'd still find him alive. While touring the hospital wards, they spotted Jack who looked very much like their son, Pierre. They joyfully claimed him as their own, and brought him home to their remote country villa in the North of France.

Jack's strange new surroundings had only added to his confusion. Before long, Alix and Gladys DuPré knew in their hearts the young wounded soldier was not their beloved Pierre. However, they'd fallen in love with him; and since Pierre was their only child, they couldn't bear to part with "him" again. When Jack started whistling his jaunty Celtic-style ditties and jigs, the DuPrés presumed him to be from Ireland or Scotland; but as Jack's speech gradually returned, they determined him to be American.

Their lovely niece, Michelle, came often to visit. Early on, she knew he wasn't Cousin Pierre, and began to have romantic feelings for the handsome stranger. She'd take him on long walks through the garden, pushing his wheelchair. Often, they rested at the edge of a pond and watched the gentle-natured Toulouse geese play in the water.

Michelle loved to tell stories of her husband, Jacques, who had fallen in one of the Flanders battles. Something about those two names struck a chord with Jack, triggering fleeting images of thundering flashes of light. Struggle as he did to fit the pieces together, there wasn't enough there to grasp onto. Michelle's eyes disclosed the secret of her heart; she was in love. However, something in Jack's subconscious would not let him give his heart in return.

Alix and Gladys had sensed "Pierre's" longing for something more than they could give, and knew it was wrong to hold him captive like a whistling, caged bird. In autumn of 1924, the Duprés finally did what was right for their beloved house guest, and reported his case to the U.S. Embassy. Still unable to walk unassisted, he was admitted to the American Hospital in Paris for evaluation, pending his return to the states. He'd later learned through a letter from Gladys, that Michelle (who could not bear to say good-bye) spent the day of his departure at the edge of the pond, watching the geese and weeping.

About that time, Jack had experienced more flickers of memory. The most commonly occurring image was of himself dancing with a beautiful brunette named Jo Jo. He asked the embassy officials to investigate the lead, but any connections to women with first names beginning with J-O who'd searched for Americans missing in action came to dead ends.

December 4th arrived. Why did the date seem so familiar to him? Jack had racked his brain until the beautiful brunette he'd often dreamed of appeared once more in his mind. Suddenly, he knew her. "My Jo Jo ... Elsie Josephine!" *Her birthday!* Tears of joy had poured from his newly enlightened eyes, realizing for the first time in seven years who he really was, and finally having the incentive he needed to fight for full recovery.

For the time being, he'd chosen not to reveal his true identity to the hospital staff or the U.S. Embassy. Seven years was a long time and a lot could have happened. If he learned Elsie had gone on with her life and remarried, he'd prefer to remain a dead man. He couldn't bear to see her with someone else. Aside from that, if he did go home he wanted to do it on his own two feet, not in a wheelchair or on crutches. Strength and mobility were rapidly returning to his limbs as his brain continued to heal, but he had more work to do.

He'd credited the swift progress he'd recently made to his tender-hearted therapist, Babette Willette, who was well-trained in working with the physically impaired. She was the mother of a profoundly handicapped son, and had developed a heart for helping others with physical challenges. Of equal value was her deep faith in God, and Jack had appreciated her prayers for healing.

Since Jack's clearance to the states was already in the works, it was merely a matter of releasing him from the hospital and booking passage on the first available ship to New York ... except he hadn't been emotionally ready to face what he might find at home.

By the end of his long story, Jack had grown weary, so Charles offered to leave and return the following morning.

After a good night's rest, the men had reminisced about the old days at Holy Infant and Charles filled Jack in on the latest news of the Sisters and the Middleton family, with one exception.

"What's that crazy little kid, Marie, up to these days?"

Charles had become silent under a noticeable dark cloud. At Jack's urging, he eventually opened up.

"Jack, after all these years, I bet you've learned to speak and read French, haven't you?"

"I'm not what you'd call fluent, Chuck, but I can carry on a halfway decent conversation and can read most of the local news. Why do you ask?"

Charles told him about Marie's poem, and reluctantly handed it over. "Just don't read it out loud, Jack. I have no desire to hear her hateful words again!"

Jack had been perplexed after reading Marie's revelation. "Chuck, how could this poem possibly be offensive to you, unless you can't *stand* the girl?"

Hollister answered with a tone of sarcasm, "How would *you* feel if Elsie said *she'd* rather be dead than be loved by you? Ironically, I've fallen for Marie, and now *I'm* the one who's been dead on the inside ever since someone translated this document. I'm an empty shell, stumbling through life's motions."

Jack had stared at him in disbelief. "Is *that* what you think this says? Quite the opposite, I assure you." Seeing Chuck's bewildered expression, he'd begun reading in English:

To My Beloved, Charles Hollister

If I had never met you,

And we were oceans apart,

There'd still be this aching longing

To hold you, in my heart.

But I've known you forever;

And though you're not far away,

Engulfing waves of fear drown out

What I struggle to say:

You're beautiful, my darling!

You're the dearest thing to me.

My love for you is fathomless—

Deeper than any sea.

I'm in love with you, Cary.

Please say you love me.

Charles had been dumbfounded and burst out with, "I can't believe my ears! Blast that conniving Jayne Blackwell! Like a horse's-you-know-what, I fell for her malicious fib hook, line and sinker! I was about to propose to the woman!" With the light of hope in his eyes, "Did I hear you right? Does it really say Marie loves me?"

"Apparently with all her heart and soul. Looks like I'm not the only proud fool around here! If this was written as recently as you think, you owe it to both of you to find out for sure."

Once the full force of reality had set in, Charles wasted no time formulating his next move. "Jack, if you can return from the dead, so can I! Whaddaya say we go home and claim our women before someone else does?!"

The authorities and hospital officials were delighted to learn of Jack's recovered memory, and lost no time in signing his release papers. Charles firmed up some business details, feeling confident he'd be bringing home enough information to get Heroes' Haberdashery off to a good start. The men had boarded the fastest possible ocean liner bound for the states on the afternoon of December 21st. Lying there now in the stateroom, staring at the ceiling, Hollister prayed the damage his follies had caused could be reversed and forgiven. All the while he'd accused Marie of being a mischievous child, she'd grown up right under his nose. How could he have so blindly misjudged her all this time, running off like a pouting adolescent every time she failed to meet his expectations?

He remembered her words at the train depot, "You *do* know how I feel about you, don't you, Cary?" It all made sense. How had he misread those words and volumes more in her wounded eyes? How she'd borne his wretched behavior was baffling. His heart swelled with love and admiration for the mature, self-controlled woman she'd become, who possessed grace and dignity beyond her tender years. "Please don't let it be too late!" *I'm the one who needs to grow up!*

Who would have dreamed that Charles Hollister and Jack O'Neill would spend the merriest of Christmases together in the middle of the Atlantic? For now, their secret was safe from family and friends. They'd be cutting it close, but would give the ladies a New Year's Eve they'd never forget!

Chapter Seventeen

December 29, 1924

She heard the door open, and he was there, like in her dreams. "Honey, I'm home!" The plate she'd been drying with a tea towel slipped through her fingers and smashed to smithereens on the hard linoleum floor as she rushed into his arms.

"Oh Jack, Jack! I *knew* you were alive. My head told me otherwise, but not my heart!" He laughed and smothered her with kisses. So many burning questions begged to be asked, but their children took precedence.

"We have to tell the kids! I can't wait for you to see each other!" Sobbing with joy, Elsie ran for the back door calling out, "Wilma! Bobby! Come here! Come here! Daddy's home!!!"

She opened her eyes, still breathless from the run, tears wet on her cheeks. *Not another dream?!* she groaned. Each one was more real! *I can't do this anymore, Jack. You have to let me go.*

Christmas had been emotionally draining, and Marie didn't have the foggiest notion of how to endure the second round of holiday festivities. Thanks to Wilma and Bobby, she had a built-in excuse for staying in on New Year's Eve. Stanley was taking Elsie to the Callahan party, and she'd be popping corn to serve the little cuties with big cups of cocoa. As usual, her thoughts were with Cary, somewhere over there, as she wondered how he'd ring out the old and ring in the new. Selfishly, she hoped he'd be as sad and lonely as she was.

Suzanne called yesterday with the exciting news she'd met a very special someone. If their relationship grew serious, she'd bring him to Coronado to meet Marie. Suz said she hoped to be as happy with her new man as Lillian and Walt were in their own magical wonderland. Marie was thrilled for her friend, knowing the challenges she'd faced while searching for her soul mate. Suz, who sought joy for others, deserved some happiness of her own. However, with a pang of guilt, she berated herself for the niggling green-eyed monster which reared its ugly head whenever someone else fell in love.

Marie took a long walk in the fresh air, hoping to clear her muddled head, and found herself automatically meandering into Tea Thyme for another heart-to-heart with Mina. Hearing how Charles had turned and walked away, not even sending her so much as a postcard, Mina openly hurt for Marie.

"I'm at a loss for words this time, Marie, but maybe a dish of my berry-filled kolaches, warm from the oven, will be of some comfort."

Marie had walked around the island until blisters formed on her heels. She dropped onto her hope chest, kicked off her shoes, and thought of the package tucked under the lid she now sat on.

She and the bright red tie where shrouded in darkness, wondering if and when he'd come to claim them ... waiting.

"Well, I can wait until the cows come home, for crying out loud, but that won't make Cary love me!" It was time to accept the fact that it was over. Marie grabbed her latest journal from the nightstand and headed for the incinerator. *The red tie is next!*

Elsie drew back the front draperies, astonished to see *another* taxi parked in front of her home. She shouted for joy, and raced to open the door. The rest of her family paraded up the walk: Mother, Father, Martha, and Frank. A shapely, beautiful blonde gripped Frank's hand ... no doubt, the famous wing walker, Connie Tanner. Marie and the kids emerged from the back of the house, and their eyes nearly popped out of their heads! Nanette jumped up from the alcove sewing machine, to warmly greet her dear friends.

"What a wonderful surprise!" Elsie cried out with tears of joy. Marie raced to squeeze Mama, while the little ones clung to their Pop Pops.

Jubilant Frank did all the explaining with a broad smile, while the others hugged, laughed, and blubbered. Proudly presenting the young woman beside him, he made the announcement they were waiting for ... "Connie and I are engaged!"

Hugh was so proud, he'd done the unimaginable: walked away from Middleton Clothiers, leaving the factory in the hands of his very capable foreman. He'd promised Anna not to talk shop until after Elsie's wedding. The family was checked in at The Del, and he invited the girls to join them there for the New Year's Eve Gala.

Hugh Middleton reached into his pocket and presented Wilma and Bobby with brightly-colored wrapped candies.

"Hugh!" his wife cautioned him. "Elsie might not want them to have sweets so late in the afternoon. It will ruin their appetites."

Hugh scoffed at her concern. "Anna, I know we're out of practice, but bear in mind that it's a grandparent's prerogative to spoil kids rotten!"

"It's okay with me," Elsie assured them. "Their tummies have been like bottomless pits lately, and I can't seem to fill them up!"

Hugh patted his adorable grandchildren on their heads, and said they'd grown like weeds. He then directed his attention to his daughters, "California obviously agrees with all of you! Looks like you're living life to its fullest, as everyone should!"

Bobby tore open his candy wrapper, broke off a piece of Bit-O-Honey, and stuffed it in his mouth. "Mmm, this is good, Pop Pops! I never had this kind before!"

"No doubt, son," Pop Pops said. "A company back home in Chicago just came out with them this year. Glad you like it!"

Elsie gave her children a firm look, "You seem to have forgotten your manners. What do you say?"

"Thank you, Pop Pops!" Wilma and Bobby chimed in unison.

Elsie noted that Wilma had been too preoccupied with Martha's Amy doll to taste her treat. She smiled as Wilma grabbed her youngest aunt's arm and led her into the hallway. "Let's go to my room, Auntie Martha, so Amy can meet my Susie!"

Bobby asked if they'd brought the dogs along, to which his grandfather replied, "Sorry, Bobby. Isabella's too old to travel, and Sibbie will be having puppies soon, so we left them in the care of a trusted friend." Of course, Bobby begged to have one of the puppies, and Pop Pops gave him a tentative promise, "Only if your mother says yes!"

Elsie finally had a chance to show off her own engagement ring, and the Middletons arranged to meet at a local Mexican restaurant that evening to welcome Stanley and Connie to the family. Elsie's heart overflowed with joy. *Could life be any sweeter?*

Anna Middleton admired the beautiful faces around the dinner table and relished the sight of her family being all together again. Her heart swelled with emotion, remembering how her son-in-law's death had cast a shadow over each of them, eventually tearing them apart. But this was a time for joy and new beginnings. Stanley Harrison was a good and kind man whom she trusted to do right by Elsie and the children.

She studied her dear little Marie, and sensed all was not well; her sparkle was gone, and there'd been no mention of Charles Hollister. She offered a silent prayer of peace and blessing upon her third born.

December 30, 1924

Anna and Marie removed the decorations from the dried-out Christmas tree, carefully packing the lights and handmade ornaments in a box to be stored in the attic.

"This task always makes me a little triste," Anna told her with misty eyes. I think of my Christmas decorations as dear friends whom I won't see for another year, and always wonder what life may bring in the months to come."

Near the end of the tree undressing project, the doorbell rang. Marie was surprised to find Jonathan Woods standing on their front porch. "There's no lesson this week, Jonathan. Did I forget to tell you?"

"Um, no. I'm not here for that." He shifted his feet, hands stuffed in his pockets, through a moment of awkward silence. *So unlike him*, Marie noted. Woods continued, "I'm wondering what you're doing for New Year's Eve. Figured Elsie and Stan will be at the Callahans' party. You going along? I'll be there, since they've invited my entire family. We all got reconnected on Christmas Eve."

Marie had no idea the Callahan and Woods families were close enough to spend holidays together, but it added up considering Jonathan and Caty's history. Not quite sure if he was asking her for a date, she hesitated. Torn between possibly hurting his feelings and the desire to be with her own family at the Gala, she knew what her answer had to be. Whether she attended the Callahan party or invited Jonathan to The Del, either way she'd be stringing him along. She had fun with him, and had even gone so far as to momentarily consider him in the running for a future mate. But he didn't make her tingle like a certain shadowy someone with a clean-shaven, dimpled chin did—the someone who was now part of her past.

She'd let Jonathan down easy for now, and break the news of her move to Chicago at his next lesson. She doubted he'd be too surprised or disappointed, since their romance had never really taken off.

"Oh Jonathan, the Callahan party sounds like loads of fun, but my family surprised us by coming to town, and we've made special plans for tomorrow night. All of us will be at the hotel, Elsie and Stanley, too. I'm so sorry we can't join you." He looked a little relieved. "Um, that's okay, Marie. I guess I can hang out with my old friend, Caty. I don't think she has a date."

A rosy flush crept from below his collar, up his neck, and onto his cheeks.

He's finally figuring it out, Marie inwardly chuckled. *Glad I let him off the hook!* "Well then, Happy New Year, Jonathan, and I'll see you next week ... I mean, year!"

With a merry laugh and bright, expectant smile, he wished her the same, adding, "Who knows what surprises 1925 has in store?!"

10:00 p.m., New Year's Eve, 1924

Charles could barely contain himself while crossing the bay. In a very short time, he'd be face-to-face with the dearest girl ... correction, *woman* ... in the world! He and Jack caught the last ferry, bringing them to the island in the nick of time to ring in the New Year.

He'd finally had a heart-to-heart with his Creator during the cruise across the Atlantic. He'd looked over the upper deck rail and watched the ship's wake churn like the turmoil in his soul. Attempts to struggle against that forceful current had submerged him deeper into a lonely abyss of arrogance and pride. He'd finally realized the futility of fighting a power greater than his own, and had surrendered to the One who could lift him from the depths of despair and set his feet on solid ground. Charles had confessed his failures, asking for mercy and strength to be all he was meant to be: a man worthy of Marie Jeannette Middleton's fathomless heart. Gone was the sullen, suspicious Charles Hollister. This was the time to not only *make* resolutions, but to commit to their fulfillment. Fear of rejection would no longer hold him back! With God's help, he'd take the bull by the horns and win the fair maiden's hand this very night! After claiming Marie as his own, the next order of business would be to finally stop procrastinating and trade in his dilapidated "Old

Girl" for a shiny new touring car. Blue would be nice, like her eyes! He could see Marie in it now, cuddled next to him on the front seat as they rode off into the land of wedded bliss. For the first time in his life, Charles Hollister believed in miracles and the power of unwavering love.

As for the newly-resurrected Jack O'Neill, he'd benefitted greatly from the past eighteen hours of recuperation since arriving in Southern California. Being the first official recipient of Heroes' Haberdashery, he looked quite dapper in the new glad rags he'd been fitted for that afternoon. Hopefully, "Jo Jo" would be too dumbfounded at the sight of him to notice the lingering limp.

Jack's only real worry was in regard to the Harrison fellow who sounded like a formidable opponent. Elsie was *his* wife (or would be, again)! No one would walk off with her if he had anything to say about it. He knew how to fight and was prepared for his greatest battle yet, if need be. Nice guy or not, he fully intended to ambush Stanley Harrison. "Like a shot out of the blue, he won't know what hit him! All is fair in love and war!"

The ferry lightly bumped against its moorings. They were home! Adrenaline pulsed through the veins of the giddy, conquering heroes who were ready to claim their prize!

The Sisters of Holy Infant signed off the old year with a traditional prayer, the *Lapsus est Annus*:

> A year is dead, a year is born;
> Thus time flies by on silent wing:
> Thou, Lord, alone canst guide our course
> And safe to heaven Thy people bring.
>
> For all past gifts we render thanks;
> For graces new we humbly pray.
> Oh, grant that we and those we love
> May ne'er from faith and duty stray.
>
> O Lord, our daily wants supply;
> Protect from sickness and disease;
> And deign to give, O God of love
> The blessings of unbroken peace.
>
> Oh, blot out all our ancient sins
> And give us strength to fall no more;
> When fight is o'er and victory won,
> Then crown us on the eternal shore.
>
> For all the old year's sins we grieve;
> Our hearts we consecrate to Thee.
> Grant us, when all our years are sped,
> Our heavenly father's face to see.

The moment Charles and Jack set foot on American soil, they'd thought it only right for their favorite nuns to be the first hearers of their incredible news. What a wonderful telephone conversation it was, hearing Jack's familiar voice for the first time in nearly a decade! The women wept for joy with praise to God, promising to keep the secret safe for the time being. They'd also thought it best to be quiet about Elsie's engagement. There was no point in upsetting the apple cart, since the future was not in their hands but in those of the Almighty.

As the bells chimed the twelfth hour, they knew the men were nearing Coronado in a time zone two hours behind their own. Oh how they'd love to be there when Elsie and Marie saw them face to face! Remaining on their knees, hand-in-hand, the devout trio thanked their Father for the miraculous gift of life, humbly submitting themselves and their loved ones to His sovereign will.

The little gray bungalow with the red door was dark when they arrived. No sign of life anywhere on the premises. The only clue obtained from the next-door neighbor was that the ladies had left an hour or so earlier, dressed up for a party.

Callahan's Cafe came to Hollister's mind, so they jumped back in the waiting taxi and headed down The Strand, only to find the diner dark, as well; a sign on the door read, "Closed December 31st and January 1st. Happy New Year!" In desperation, they made a mad dash for the Callahan residence, and were relieved to find the joint jumpin' with lights, voices and music.

Jonathan Woods and Cathleen Callahan sipped on cider frappes while watching the other party revelers hop and toddle to the lively Lindy Hop blaring from Paddy's Victrola. Jonathan

couldn't keep his eyes off his ex-girlfriend. She was a knock-out in her Kelly green dropped-waist number; a sprig of mistletoe was artfully tucked in her lustrous brown hair. Finally mustering the nerve, "Say, Caty with a C ... mind if I give ya a whirl?"

With sparkling eyes, Caty exuberantly replied, "Aye, Jonathan! I thought ya'd naiver ahsk!" The couple whirled past the front door as Charles Hollister stepped through it with a strange man—eyes darting about the room.

Pausing, then dancing in place, Jonathan asked, "Lookin' for someone, Mr. Hollister?"

Scanning the crowded parlor, Hollister answered, "We are. Have you seen Elsie and Marie? I figured they'd be here."

"Well," Jonathan answered breathlessly, "they were invited, but went to the big, fancy shindig at The Del."

With a glance at his wristwatch, Hollister muttered something to his companion as they dashed out the door. Jonathan and Caty moved on, smilin' and whirlin' the magical night away.

The Grand Ballroom, Hotel del Coronado

Feeling like Cinderella without Prince Charming, Marie soaked in the elegant atmosphere of the Grand Ball Room. All dressed up in her sweet little "Alice Blue Gown" with beaded for-get-me-nots and no one to enamor, seemed pointless; nonetheless, there she sat like a piece of fine furniture. The creamy-white decor, shimmering chandeliers hanging from the lofty ceiling, and the enormity of the room made her feel small and insignificant in the vast scheme of things. There was gaiety all around, but as much as she loved her family and this beautiful wooden palace, her heart just wasn't in it. She regretted all the times she'd resented Cary's annoying hovering, but it was better this way. Seeing him now would only bring heartache. It also made her sad to think how much she'd miss visiting this beautiful place after going home with Mama and Pops in a few weeks.

Frank and Connie were in their own blissful dreamland, gazing into each other's eyes; Stanley and Elsie had their heads together, planning their future, no doubt; Mama and Pops regally strutted around the dance floor; and even Auntie Madge and Nanette LaNell were cutting a rug with dapper gents. Marie had seen Winifred Britton arrive with the family of John D. Spreckels, entrepreneur and controller of the Coronado Beach Company. She'd guessed that Winnie was sweet on Stanley, and took pity on her, hoping she'd find the happiness she deserved. And of course, there was Jayne Blackwell, dressed in slinky gold lame, on the hunt for someone ... Cary, no doubt. For that reason alone, she was glad he wasn't there.

Mama and Pops returned to the table, to give their aching feet and backs a rest. With a sly gleam in his eye, Pops whispered something in his demure wife's ear, which made Mama blush and scold with a girlish giggle, "Well, *Huuugh!*" Noting his daughter's melancholy mood, "Why so glum, Kiddo?" Pops asked. Then with a teasing grin, "Eat a ..."

"*banana!*" Marie chimed in. "It will make you feel better! I didn't see those on the menu, Pops," she laughed, feeling a little better. Leave it to him to cheer her up with his predictable wisecracks!

Marie got a kick out of watching Mama observe Miss Blackwell with a slight smirk, as Jayne sashayed past their table in her usual affected manner, stuffed like a *saucisson* (sausage) in her shimmery gown. "Stars! That's rare!" Her mother's comment caused Marie to stifle a giggle with her linen napkin.

In the last few minutes of 1924, lovers sought out their mates, anticipating the stroke of midnight kiss. Peeking under the white table cloth, Marie considered hiding until it was all over; to witness all the gooey romance would be unbearable. Sometimes life wasn't fair. She wished Wilma, Bobby, and Martha were here to keep her company, but they were having a "jolly good time" at Grandma Gable's.

Seconds later, Marie heard a gasp which drew her attention toward her sister. Stanley was supporting Elsie, whose legs seemed to have gone out from under her. Elsie looked like she'd seen a ghost, and was pointing a shaky finger at something on the opposite side of the room. Fearing it might, indeed, *be* the famous ghost of the Hotel del Coronado, Marie followed Elsie's gaze, nearly fainting, herself. "Cary?!" And who was the man with him? *It couldn't be...!*

Suddenly, Elsie tore from Stanley's firm grip and raced across the floor, as the slightly-stooped handsome man dropped his cane and took tentative steps in her direction. Within inches of each other, they stopped, breathlessly gazing in wonder. Marie heard Elsie ask with a quavering voice, "Are you real?" He answered with a confident smile, "Yes, Jo Jo honey, I'm real! Let me prove it to you!" He held out a perfect, single red rose. "Oh Jack, *Jack* my love!" Elsie cried, as she melted into his arms.

Marie cast a swift glance toward Stanley, who'd collapsed into the nearest chair, holding his bewildered head in his hands. *Poor, sweet Stanley.* She empathized with him. Then, Winifred Britton cautiously approached, gently placing her hand upon his heaving shoulder.

Her heart in her throat, Marie's eyes shot back to Cary, who was marching straight for her. She stood and took a faltering step toward him. No Gish Glide tonight; her knees felt like rubber as the reality of all that had taken place within seconds sunk in.

Marie gasped when Jayne Blackwell spotted Hollister and tried to intercept. "*There* you are, you naughty boy! Where have you been hiding yourself?!"

Charles completely ignored Jayne. His eyes were trained directly on his goal as he advanced with the purposeful stride of a man on a mission. He stopped a few feet from Marie with the light of dawn dancing in his beautiful ebony eyes. She could tell he was different somehow ... a glowing transformation. What was in his hand? A rumpled sheet of paper?

He smiled broadly and spoke, "I picked up a little French while I was away." On closer inspection, Marie nearly stopped breathing. He was holding the love poem she'd written on the beach nearly two months ago. *He knows!* Searching each other's eyes, the truth was silently revealed.

Her heart pounded wildly as he crushed her against his strong, musky-scented frame, cupped her delicate chin in the palm of his hand, and lowered his hungry lips to her trembling ones. Amidst blaring party horns, falling confetti and the crackle of fireworks, they kissed firmly and deeply. She positively tingled! They pulled slightly apart, and tears of joy streamed from two sets of eyes: sky blue and coal black. She shyly pressed a fingertip into the dent she'd so longed to touch, and kissed him again.

He nuzzled her neck and hoarsely whispered the words she'd waited to hear, "Bonjour, Mimi. *Je t'aime* (I love you)!"

Smiling radiantly into his yearning eyes, she softly caressed his smooth, burning cheek. "Bonjour, Mon Amour!"

La Fin

Epilogue

January, 1925

As much as I admire my Pops, I beg to differ with him on one crucial point. Swallowing a boatload of bananas would *not* have made my broken heart feel better. The only cure for what ailed me was having Cary's strong arms wrapped snugly around me, while his starving lips nearly devoured my own. He took my breath away with that very first kiss ... and much to my delight, takes advantage of every possible opportunity to make me tingle over and over again!

Mama, on the other hand, was right when she said, "This, too, shall pass." My agonizing days of waiting for the assurance of Cary's love have passed by and are becoming a faded memory. At last, Cary is all mine. The proof of it flashes on my left hand: an exquisite two-carat Cartier rose-cut "sparkler!" I nearly died of laughter when he confessed to seeing me with Brad at the Boathouse that August afternoon, thinking we were engaged!

That didn't come close to his shock over the whopper Jayne Blackwell told him with her deliberately twisted translation of my love poem. He swears he was never in love with Jayne—cross his heart, an' hope ta die! According to our very reliable source and eye witness, Auntie Madge, Miss Blackwell was last seen storming from the Grand Ballroom in a deluge of tears. We can only surmise she no longer finds our "clime" appealing, and has sashayed even farther south for the remainder of "the season" where she is, no doubt, honing in on her next conquest. To tell the truth, I can't help feeling a little sorry for her, and pray she will one day find what she's searching for.

The joy Cary and I now share plays second fiddle to Jack and Elsie's incredible reunion on New Year's Eve. The shred of hope Elsie kept alive within her spirit and dreams manifested itself in the surprise appearance of Jack O'Neill ... in the flesh! None of us slept a wink that night: laughing, crying, hugging, and catching up with Jack on the lost years. The incredible story of how Jack's whistling led to his being found by Cary was nothing short of Divine intervention! Elsie had blushed and giggled when she described the ecstasy of their reunion kiss. She said her toes literally curled and bells rang! Maybe tingly lasts forever, after all!

Though the required seven-year waiting period expired in November, Jack's official death certificate had never been processed, leaving him and Elsie legally free to resume their marriage from where they left off. Jack and Bobby instantly fell in love with each other: Jack said Bobby is everything he'd dreamed his son would be, and Bobby was so proud of his real-live, American hero Daddy that he nearly burst his buttons! Jack couldn't take his eyes off his little "Woochie," seeing how Wilma had grown into a smart and self-confident little girl, who was the spitting image of his dear departed mother, Molly. He delighted in watching Willie imitate my signature Gish Glide from dawn to dusk, practicing for her upcoming role as Flower Girl.

The four O'Neills are now on their way back to Chicago with the rest of the family and Nanette, to reclaim their former life and raise the kids among a large number of loved ones. What a wonderful reunion it will be when Jack returns to Holy Infant! It was agonizing to let go of Wilma and Bobby, but they have the undivided attention of their adoring Auntie Martha now, and everything is as it was meant to be. Mama's next letter will, no doubt, be fun to read!

As much as I'll miss my big sister and her family, it's better for Elsie and Stanley to be 2,000 miles apart, eliminating the painful possibility of bumping into each other. Elsie had fallen for Stanley, proving it *is* possible to be in love with two people at the same time. Their separation has, of course, been harder on Stanley. Cary and I met Mr. Harrison walking Becket at Star Park yesterday. The deep sadness in his eyes was heartwrenching. It was so strange for the two of us to stand there, thinking how close we came to being brother and sister. We spoke briefly, and Stanley mentioned a planned spring mission's trip to the Congo with Winifred Britton. It sounds like an exciting adventure to me, and the anticipation of the trip gives Stanley new direction for his future. He seems to be a man of deep faith with a heart for lost souls. In fact, according to Elsie, Stanley has been writing to Avery Weston in prison, sharing God's love and forgiveness with him. Selflessly, Mr. Harrison expressed his sincere joy for Jack and Elsie, believing in God's sovereign will. He's an extraordinary man, and I can see what attracted Elsie to him. All this time, Winnie has been waiting in the wings. I pray the Lord will guide and bless them through life's mysterious and unpredictable journey.

Bobby can't wait for Sibbie to deliver her English Cocker Spaniel pups in a few more weeks, and has been promised the pick of the litter. It must be a male, of course. Although he's not allowed to name it his favorite word, "Pooh," he's settled for "Puddles."

Prior to the O'Neill family's departure, the keys to the little gray beach bungalow were handed over to the new owner, Charles Hollister! He'll carry me over its threshold this summer. In the meantime, while Cary is refurbishing the place, Mildred Gable has offered me a room in her lovely Victorian. She says that Cary is more than welcome to visit, so long as there's "no hanky-panky!" She must think we're a couple of impulsive teenagers, for crying out loud!

Auntie Madge, Tante Arletta, and Suz will be our chaperones while traveling in Cary's snazzy 1925 Cobalt Blue Chevrolet Touring Car to Chicago, where we will tie the knot at Holy Name Cathedral, one week after Frank and Connie's ceremony. Our reception will be hosted in Mama and Pop's back yard, in the shade of the sprawling oak tree—where unbeknown to us at the time, Cary and I first fell in love.

At Cary's request, my matron of honor Elsie, accompanied by my second attendant, Suz, will delight our guests with her rendition of "You Made Me Love You" from the open window overlooking Mama's rose garden.

Following our wedding feast of leg of lamb, I've planned a special dessert for my husband: a double-dip chocolate ice cream cone! Cary plans to mail an invitation to his father's last known address, with the hope of Raymond Hollister (and possibly Cary's half sister, Caroline) doing us the great honor of attending our wedding. The invitation list also includes Mirin and a few other "kids" Cary grew up with at Holy Infant. I'm looking forward to meeting them!

Suz and the aunts will return to California by rail, while Mr. and Mrs. Charles Basil Hollister of Coronado, California enjoy a leisurely road trip on their way home. We know our honeymoon will never be over, but at some point we *will* need to come down to earth and get on with the exciting plans God has for us. Cary will be hard at work over-seeing the San Diego headquarters of Heroes Haberdashery, while I continue to teach at home, studying at the San Diego School of Music and Dance, and eventually establish a small orchestra for local adult string musicians: The Coronado Community Symphony. It will be the first of its kind along The Silver Strand, and my way of making Pop's dream for me come true.

"Uncle Chuck" finally kept his promise and took the kids and their father on a little sailing excursion before they left town. A crew is now at work sprucing up the Solitaire, which will officially be re-christened the "Marie" on my 21st birthday, three weeks from today. In case you're wondering, Elsie rescued my scorched journal from the incinerator, and used her big sister powers of persuasion to prevent me from tossing in the tie box. We engaged in a shouting match like the old days, but Elsie won and I'm glad she did. Red is Cary's color!

Looking back over the past 10 months, I laugh at my former self: the cocky, headstrong young girl who didn't want a man in her life! Just when we think we're in control, God in His great wisdom, grace, and even humor, steps in and turns things topsy-turvy, molding us and preparing us for His perfect plan. The people I've met in Coronado, from different backgrounds and cultures, have enriched my life: Mina, Jonathan, the Callahans, Mildred Gable, Mitzie and Paolo, the mischievous Arnold Wilcox, and even my rival, Jayne Blackwell! Nothing happened by chance, but by Divine Providence; every relationship and detail as intricately woven together as the vines of Elsie's Creeping Charlie. God makes no mistakes.

I may never fully master the task of governing "my kingdom" well, as Louisa May Alcott longed to do; but with God's help, I'll become the woman He created me to be, and a worthy helpmate for my dark, dimpled darling—my very own "Mr. Darcy!" Although Cary is more than pleased with his grown-up "Mimi," he affectionately says that to him I'll always be the wide-eyed little girl dangling by her knees in the oak tree.

As Mama said while putting away the Christmas decorations, we wonder what life may bring in the months ahead; but with Cary at my side, I can't wait to find out!

How do I spell love? F-A-M-I-L-Y.

Dieu vous bénisse, chéries! Marie

Dear All Family Recipes

Suz's Orange Nummy

Ingredients:

- 1 (11-ounce) can mandarin oranges (drained)
- 1 (8 ounce) can pineapple (drained)
- 1 (6 ounce) package orange-flavored Jell-O
- 1 pint cottage cheese (small curd)
- 1 (8 ounce) container Cool Whip, thawed

In a large bowl, mix fruit and dry Jell-O. Add the cottage cheese, and then fold in Cool Whip. Chill at least one hour before serving.

Mina's Kolache

Ingredients:

- 1 cup butter, room temperature
- 1 (8 ounce) package cream cheese
- 1/4 teaspoon vanilla
- 1/2 teaspoon salt

2 1/4 cup flour

thick jam or fruit filling (e.g., apricot or raspberry).

1. Cream butter and cream cheese until fluffy, beat in vanilla

2. Combine flour and salt; add in fourths to butter mixture, blending well after each addition. Chill dough until easy to handle.

3. Roll dough to 3/8 thickness on a floured surface. Cut out 2 inch circles & place on ungreased cookie sheets.

4. Make a "thumbprint" about 1/4 inch deep in each cookie and fill with jam. Bake at 350 degrees 10-12 minutes until delicately browned on edges.

Mina's Cucumbers and Sour Cream

Ingredients:

4 long, green cucumbers, peeled and sliced green onions, finely chopped (to taste)

2 Tablespoons vinegar

3/4 cup sour cream (not low fat)

1/3 cup Kosher salt

pepper (to taste).

In glass bowl alternate slices of cucumber with Kosher salt & vinegar. Cover bowl with plastic wrap and chill 3 to 4 hours, then drain cucumbers well in a colander. Add onions, sour cream, and pepper (to taste). Refrigerate until ready to serve.

Auntie Madge's Raisin Pie

Ingredients:

2 cups raisins

2 cups water

½ cup sugar

2 tablespoon cornstarch

¼ teaspoon salt

1 tablespoon lemon juice

1 tablespoon butter or margarine

1 9-inch double pie crust

Combine raisins and water in a small saucepan. Bring for 5 minutes. Blend sugar, cornstarch, and salt into the raisin mixture. Remove from heat and stir in lemon juice and butter. Cool slightly. Turn raisin mixture onto bottom crust of lined pastry pan, and top with second crust (latticed).

Bake at 425° for 30 to 35 min.

About the Author

Born and raised in the Chicago area, Linda wrote her first poem at the age of nine, and has always enjoyed the art of self-expression through the written word.

Linda Corrigan Baker, an evangelical Christian, resides in Southern California and finds fulfillment in her roles of mother, grandmother, and school district secretary. She considers this season of life to be one of the best, successfully finishing her first half marathon and publishing her first work, *Dear All*, in the past year. She also keeps active with bi-weekly Zumba sessions.

Mrs. Baker is grateful to her family and friends (some of whom are portrayed as characters in *Dear All*) for their loving encouragement and support during the creation of this faith-based love story.

Life is often filled with daunting challenges and overwhelming sorrows, but Linda can attest that through faith in Jesus Christ, all things are possible.

Visit her at: www.Facebook.com/Linda.Corrigan.Baker
www.lindacorriganbaker.weebly.com
https://twitter.com/lcbDearAll